Darkness Demons and Light

A collection of short stories

Ted Tillotson

Darkness – Demons and Light

Published by Dragon Lair Books

Avenal, California

http://www.tedtillotsondragonlairbooks.com

Cover design by
Dragon Lair Books

Book design by Lord Dragon

ISBN: 978-0615579429

Printed in the United States of America

Also By Ted Tillotson

Available on Amazon.com and other retail outlets

Deathmaker – a dark psychological thriller

**Published by Omega Publications
Palm Springs, CA**

* * * *

The Magic Meadow
Kayla's fantasy

**Published by
Dragon Lair Books**

Avenal, California

* * * *

Thorns of the Rose

* * * *

For my late wife,

Barbara

1949 - 2008

* * * *

Many thanks to my proof reader,

Marcia K. Feese

Her keen eyes are priceless.

* * * *

Table of contents

Introduction

The Darkness

About the Author

Introduction

The Darkness

I am the womb in which the seeds of evil are
conceived.
I give birth to the demons and beasts that live in
nightmares.
I am the deceit and hate that breeds in the black
depths
of the murderer's heart.
I am the Darkness.
I live with vermin and mold beneath rotting cellar
stairs.
I fill the empty cistern where the light of day dare
not touch.
My shroud covers the filth of wet alleys and
gutters in
the dead of night.
I hide the fallen man who shivers at the door
of his own death.
I am the Darkness.
I am welcomed by men and women of the night.
They sing and dance and sell their souls. I am
the guardian of their sins.
Children fear my chilling touch.
Thieves embrace my presence while the blind
curse my existence.
I am the Darkness.
No man is immune to me. I live in every
human heart.
I am the absence of light, of faith and hope.
I fill the universe.
I am the Darkness.

Darkness – Demons and Light

Death is the Hunter

*J*ennifer's painful screams echoed off the wet, stone walls of the abandoned winery. Her terrified cries were lost in the deep shadows of the basement chamber.

Simm grinned, raised his arms and looked up at the large painting above his makeshift altar. "The woman's terror, pain and blood are for you, my Masters."

It was a work of oil by an unknown artist. Simm had purchased the painting from a musty old shop that sold used and rare books. He paid fifty-dollars without hesitation. He was delighted. The proprietor had said, "You may wish you had never made this purchase."

Simm had laughed and left the dingy, dark shop with the find of his life.

Now, he gestured in reverence to the image of a beast with four heads. Each grotesque face glared back at him from the dark canvas. Simms believed he could see them move in the shadows the artist had so giftedly painted. He was excited, aroused by the images.

"My Master, you are the path to my destiny–I serve you with all of my soul!"

Simm pushed the point of his dagger into the flesh of Jennifer's naked chest and cut the shape of an inverted cross. He loved the sound of her screams. He became more excited. Her agony thrilled him more than having his way with her.

The four demon heads glared down from the painting.

Simm's blood ran hot. He shook with desire beyond the anticipation of having Jennifer again– after she was dead.

* * * *

Anita Webster cried out in ecstasy. She rolled onto her left side, snuggled against Larry and lifted her glass of brandy. "Another toast," she whispered.

Larry smiled. He loved her softness and warmth. "That's three so far."

Anita raised her snifter toward the crackling fire. "One for suggesting that we do it in front of the fireplace. The second for the way we did it. And the third–this one, to your success."

Larry touched his glass to hers and bit her gently on the neck. "You're the reason I've accomplished anything."

Anita sipped her drink and relaxed into Larry's arms.

* * * *

Simm licked fresh blood from the blade of his dagger and smiled up at the picture of the four-headed beast. "For you … always for you. I will bring you all the sinners!"

The images moved.

Simm closed his eyes and smiled. He reached up and touched the inscription in the lower right corner of the painting. He whispered it. "I am and shall always be."

The four heads looked down at him. Simm felt their red eyes. "I know … I'm your servant. I will bring you all the blackened souls I can find."

Jennifer cried out again, begging. "Oh, God–please!"

Simm became instantly angry. "God? You bitch!" He pressed the blade against her throat. "That name is never spoken here!" He sliced open a small cut. Jennifer struggled helplessly against her restraints and sobbed.

Simm dug his weapon into the rough wood of the altar. He pulled back the hood of his black robe and gritted his teeth and hissed, "I'm giving you to them, the kings of darkness." Simm grinned up at the painting. "She will be yours!"

Young Jennifer fought against the leather straps. She turned her head away. "God, please help me!"

Simm pulled his dagger free from the altar and raised it to the painting of the four-headed beast. "She cries the name of God in our presence. It is blasphemy! I give her black soul to you." He plunged the dagger deep into Jennifer's fragile chest. The young woman made a desperate, wet groan. Her eyes froze, wide open, blood gushed from her mouth.

The images in the painting stared down at him.

He shuddered. "I'm sorry, my kings. Jennifer wasn't right. The others weren't either." He bowed beneath the painting. "Forgive me. I will make the offering pure." He dared not look at the beasts. Head down and eyes closed he said, "I promise, I will find the right gift."

Simm bowed again before the ominous painting of the beasts. "I promise you worthy sinners, my Lords and I shall deliver them unto you." He took the lethal, twelve-inch dagger from the altar. Simm smiled at the thought of what he was about to do. He blinked his cold, gray eyes into Jennifer's dead stare. You're going away now, little princess. I'm sending you to meet our king, the Lord of Darkness, and the ruler of death." Simm's face contorted into a mask of evil. He raised the dagger and plunged it into Jennifer's body again and again.

The four heads returned to a still image on the cold canvas.

* * * *

Anita lifted up on her left elbow and kissed Larry's warm back. "That was the absolute best way to get the morning going." She rubbed her sleep-filled eyes and fell back into the softness of their bed. "I love you." Her words were satisfied whispers.

The fine fabric of the window curtains rustled on a gentle breeze and allowed brief streams of morning sun to dance across the bedroom.

Larry sat on the edge of the bed. He lit a cigarette. "In a way," he chuckled, "Being gone for a while will be good for my health."

"What?" She turned toward him.

He faced her and stroked her thick, brown hair. "Between last night and this morning, you've taken all my strength away." His face glowed with loving expression. "I need time to recharge." He kissed her on the forehead, nose and lips. "I love you too."

Anita laughed. "We'd save time if we showered together."

"You first, love. I couldn't handle another encounter."

Displaying herself in a model-like pose she

whispered, "You're passing up a great body here."
She shivered and slipped into her robe.

"You cold?"

"Just a chill. I'll close the window."

Larry hugged her. "I'll get it. You take
your shower first."

Something cold and dark crossed Anita's
heart. "Yeah, I'll hit the shower."

* * * *

Simm pulled himself away from the cold
corpse of Jennifer Corey. Disoriented for a
moment, he shuddered at the body beneath him.
He had fallen into a deep sleep after having her
twice. He looked up, focused on the image in the
painting and remembered. A shudder ran through
him.

"My Lords, forgive me for falling asleep in
your sight." He turned away and removed his
black robe. "I've sinned again ... I beg your
forgiveness." Simm raised his arms to the evil
images. "When I've completed my special mission,
you'll wash me clean of all sin–I know you will."
He studied the faces of the painted demons a
moment longer. "Jennifer's soul wasn't right. I'll
find the right one–I promise"

He lifted the ravaged remains of the young
woman from the bloodstained altar and carried
her to the edge of the pit. A foul vapor rose from

its black depths. Simm threw Jennifer into the oily darkness.

The four heads of the beast looked down upon Simm with contempt.

* * * *

Anita hugged Larry again when his flight was announced for the second time. "You touch one hair on one head of one model and I'll slice off your manhood so fast you won't even feel it."

He laughed "You're the only woman I'll ever touch." His voice became serious. "Anita, you're the only female I want in my private life. Those other girls are hired subjects, nothing more. They're assignments–that's it." He kissed her. "If it weren't for you, I wouldn't have this shoot." Larry shook his head. "I wish you'd at least think about modeling professionally."

She pressed a finger to Larry's lips. "I'm a teacher, not a model." She kissed him. "I'll pose for you privately. That's a turn on for us only."

He smiled. "What pose will you strike when I get back?"

I've got ten days to think about it, but I can tell you it will be wicked." She hugged him again and blinked away her tears. "I love you."

"I love you, Ms. Anita."

"Me too. Now get on your damn plane and fly away."

* * * *

Simm poured more bottled water into the large bowl he used as a wash basin. He scrubbed his face vigorously, then his hands. "I'll be ready soon, my Lords." He combed his hair, leaned forward and stared into the reflection of his handsome face. "Your time is coming, Simm," He smiled and studied his perfect teeth. "Damn, what a dazzling smile you have." Simm dried his hands again and combed his golden hair once more.

His Christian name was Thomas Farley, the son of the Reverend, Albert Farley, a Bible-beating preacher who beat his wife to death with a framing-hammer fifteen years ago.

The good reverend was now doing thirty years to life at Vacaville in Northern California.

The good preacher had beaten the good-word into young Tom, literally, with the good-book itself.

The Lord's word hadn't set too well with Thomas after his mother's brutal murder. Young Tom took to the darker side of religion. Then, a little more than a boy, Thomas made a pact with the prince of darkness, the ruler of hell–the ultimate demon, Satan himself.

Thomas Farley sounded like hell. Young Tom thought about that for a time. He made up a name.

S.I.M.M.

"Satan Is My Master–what a great handle. I love it."

Thomas repeated it over and over. "Simm, Simm, Simm! It fits. Satan-is-my-master!"

"What a name. What a great faith."

Simm went to a cabinet on the far side of his room. He put away his dagger and smiled. "I'll need you again soon."

His home was a twenty-by-twenty-foot loft on the second floor of the winery. There, he washed, slept and ate.

Simm grinned at himself as he passed another mirror. "I've given twenty-four sin-filled souls to them. Now, I must find the perfect offering."

* * * *

During the drive back from the airport, Anita thought about her plans for the next ten days. She chuckled to herself in the memory of Larry's comments: *I suppose you and Kirsten will shop yourselves to death and see more movies than Roger Ebert.*

"Yes," she had replied. "We will."

She took 'G' street out of downtown San Diego and headed East on the 125 freeway. It was October, which in Southern California didn't seem much different from December or June, except for seasonal events.

Anita and Kirsten, her fellow elementary school teacher, planned to spend a good part of that Saturday in La Mesa. They would attend the rollicking, crowded, noisy Oktoberfest. The event was an over-priced street bazaar jammed with booths of over-priced crafts, kegs of German beer and enough bratwurst and sauerkraut to feed a legion.

The Fest, as they called it, was an event Anita and Larry had enjoyed every year for the five they had been together. It was a way to be with Larry in spirit.

* * * *

Simm could hardly contain his excitement. He stood before the steaming pit staring into the blackness. "I will find the right souls my King," he whispered. Thrilled with the thought, he looked up at the painting of the demon of four heads. "I pray that you'll grant me a place at your side. There, I shall worship you for eternity." Simm bowed and turned away from the piercing eyes of the four heads.

He was pleased with himself.

The evil images grinned.

* * * *

By ten-thirty Kirsten and Anita had eaten two ears of corn-on-the-cob, barbecued in the shuck, and consumed one pint each of dark, German beer.

Anita said, "I miss him already."

"None of that. We're having fun."

"Yeah, but I do miss him."

Kirsten wiped her mouth with a paper napkin and wrapped her chewed corn cob into it. "Let's walk off this stuff and hit the booths."

"In a few minutes. I'm enjoying the moment."

"You're daydreaming about Larry."

"Yeah, I am."

* * * *

Simm glanced back toward the pit with disgust. He had thrown the bodies of three men into the thick darkness. "For you I have nothing but contempt." He turned. "You're the worst of the lot–the least of my offerings."

He hated the men he had taken. They had come to him by default. Each one had gotten in the way. They weren't part of his plan for the King of Four Heads. He walked back to his altar and raised his clean hands to the painting. "My Masters–I promise you, this day I shall find the perfect offering."

The image of the four-headed beast remained as it was, a painting on a large canvas.

Harry Fell, came to mind. A fat-bellied private detective chasing after young Sandy Wallace, Simm's first gift. "Worship the Masters, you bastard!" His words bounced off the wet walls of the chamber. He had hacked at the detective with a hatchet. Still screaming, the private cop resisted. Simm laughed and kicked the man into the steaming pit. "You're not a worthy sacrifice, Harry!"

Young Sandy was. What an excellent demonstration of the commitment. She was young and filled with sin. Her life-force was so strong she was also still alive when he threw her into the dark. The girl was a fantastic *high*.

Simm enjoyed the memory. He had taken her several times and beat her repeatedly. "She kept screaming–such glorious terror."

There were twenty other women and four men. He loved the memories of all the females. Each one was like a treasure to him, but he hadn't pleased the four-headed demon–not yet.

He knelt before his altar and looked up at the four heads. "Today, my Lords. Today, I will bring you my ultimate offering."

* * * *

Kirsten and Anita sat in silence sipping from their fresh cups of cold beer. Anita said, "How's it going with you and Greg?"

"Greg makes excellent dinner conversation, he's a perfect date. We read books together, he's got position, money, good looks and he's fantastic in bed."

"You've just described the perfect man."

"Greg can't stand kids or animals–my four cats hate him." She took another sip of beer. "My life is full of wonderful, screaming children. That's why I teach. I love those brats. I want a batch of my own." She looked at Anita. "Does that make sense?"

"I didn't know you and Greg weren't working."

"We are … except for the damn cats and kids." Sudden tears appeared. She wiped them away. "Maybe I'll meet a real bastard who loves kids and cats."

Anita hugged her. "That would serve you right."

* * * *

Simm jingled Jennifer's car keys and smiled. "I'll find the perfect offering today." He renewed his vow to the painted masters. "Soon, my Lords, I will be worthy of your reward." He shook with excitement. "My offering will be complete. The power of that black soul will open the door to your kingdom. I shall come to you in glory."

The spoken words made his heart pump rapidly. His blood surged hot through his veins. He felt powerful, aroused. "Today. I will find the key to the gate!"

A hissing sound came up from the pit.

Putrid fumes rolled up into the chamber.

More hissing with low, guttural tones.

Simm went to the edge of the hole and looked into the dark. He heard a faint, wet sound and caught a flash of light. It was gone in an instant.

Fire, he thought. *It was fire.*

"I'm off, my Masters. Off to Oktoberfest."

* * * *

Kirsten and Anita touched their cups together in one of many toasts. Kirsten said, "To all the noisy kids everywhere!"

Anita added, "And to all the lovely cats in the whole wide world."

They laughed quite loud. Kirsten shouted, "To all kids and cats!"

Simm stood in line at a nearby beer-booth and heard the laughter, cheers and chatter of the two young women. It excited him. *Have I found her?* He focused on Anita. *That one has the right look. The masters would be pleased.* His blood ran hot again. *Is she the one?* He watched the two women and started developing a plan.

He bought a large cup of beer and found a table near the two ladies.

A voice in Simm's head startled him. *Are you sure you've chosen well, Mr. Simm, the master would not be pleased if you haven't.* The voice was hollow and ragged.

His mind raced. Other messages had come before, but they were in his own voice. *"Who are you?"* He whispered the question and looked around to see if anyone had heard.

I am Raven. Like you, I serve the dark Majesty. I've come to tell you, your time is near.

"When? How soon?" This time he spoke out loud.

Kirsten and Anita glanced at him and then resumed their conversation.

A cold trickle of sweat crept down Simm's neck from behind his left ear. He shuddered. The voice in his head was gone.

Anita took the last swallow of beer from her cup. "That's it. No more, I'm driving."

Kirsten said, "Yeah, me too. However, dear friend, Greg's taking me to a fantastic dinner at Tom Hamm's tomorrow and I don't need to be hung over for that."

"Maybe you do."

Polka music blasted from a nearby bandstand and covered all conversations.

Simm could see they were finishing their drinks and laughing. "Bitches ... I'll take both of you," he whispered. "You won't be laughing when I get you on the altar." He gulped down half of his beer.

The women left their table. Anita said, "Let's blow a few bucks at the booths before we leave."

"That's what we came here to do, I guess."

The crowd made good cover. Simm walked behind them as the two women poked through a few booths and made purchases. *Spend all your money now, ladies, he thought. It's your last shopping spree.* This was the day, his time had arrived.

At the last booth Anita found a prize. "Will you look at this–it's an omen!" She held up an audio tape and giggled.

"What is it?"

"It's Moody Blues–*Knights in White Satin.*"

"Okay, great album. So what?"

Anita bought the tape. "Larry loves Moody Blues. He can play it in the car when he's on the road." She put the cassette in her shopping bag. "You remember the poem at the end of 'Satin?'

"Yeah, I do … it goes, Breathe deep, the gathering gloom. Watch lights fade from every room."

Anita picked up the verse. "Bed-sitter people look back and lament. Another day's useless energy spent."

Kirsten said, "God, I love it. We're both acting like teenagers here."

They left the shopping area and headed toward the parking lot.

Simm followed, he was driven now. *Control, Simm, stay in control and be sure you're right.* It was the voice of Raven again.

"Yes, control." He walked quickly to

Jennifer's Honda, opened the trunk and uncovered his .45 automatic. He shoved the gun into his belt and closed the trunk. The women had stopped by a car three rows away. He smiled.

Anita leaned into the back of her bright red Nissan 300-ZX. Kirsten stood beside her.

Simm came up behind them. "Excuse me. Do you have a set of jumpers?"

Kirsten turned around to face him. He was good-looking, lean and tall. A lock of blond hair bobbed over his forehead and his smile was pleasant. She grinned and brushed her hair as if she suddenly wanted it to look better. "Do you, Anita?"

Still leaning into the back of the car, Anita said, "No, I don't"

With a flash of nickel-plating, Simm pressed the .45 into Kirsten's right side. "Forget it, bitch!"

Anita jerked her head out of the car and saw the gun. "My God!"

Simm put his left arm around Kirsten's neck and shoved himself against Anita pinning her to the back of the car. "Do what I tell you or I'll blow this lady's guts all over the parking lot."

Kirsten's eyes went wide with fear. She stiffened in Simm's grip. "What do you want?"

"Shut the fuck up!" He bumped himself against Anita. "You get in the passenger seat now!" He stepped away from the rear of the car and stared at Anita through his cold gray eyes.

"Make one wrong move and you're both dead. Are we clear on that?"

Anita nodded and pulled the keys from the trunk lock and moved toward the passenger side of the car. She fumbled with the keys. "Oh, God!"

"Get it open, cunt!" Simm pushed the business end of the automatic harder into Kirsten's side. To her he said, "Now you and me will waltz to the driver's door and you'll slide into the back nice and easy, right?"
"Yes."

"Good for you, bitch!"

Anita slid into the passenger seat and started to cry. "Why are you doing this?"

"Shut up, and buckle in." He brought the muzzle of the .45 up under Kirsten's chin. "Squeeze your sexy ass into the back seat real slow."

Kirsten nodded and sobbed. "Please, we didn't do anything to you."

"Doesn't matter. You've been selected." He slammed the pistol against the right side of her head twice. She fell across the seat unconscious and bleeding.

Anita cried out and held her hands against the sides of her face. "Please don't hurt us."

Simm laughed. "Your hurt has only just begun. He whacked Anita across the back of her head. She slumped forward and passed out.

"Good, now we can go home."

* * * *

Less than an hour later Simm had lighted fifty black candles and had prepared the altar. Kirsten would be the first in his double sacrifice to the Beast of Four Heads.

"This is the night of ascension!" Simm's voice echoed off the damp walls. "You, in spirit and I in body will pass through the door of darkness."

Kirsten stirred. She cried out, "Anita." Her voice sounded weak and filled with pain. "Oh God, Anita."

Simm shuddered. He reached down and grabbed a handful of Kirsten's hair. "Never speak that name in this temple–do you hear me?" He slammed her head against the crude altar several times. He raised his arms to the painting of the beast. "I'm about to prepare my final offerings. Together they will be perfect."

Anita came to and started fighting against the ropes Simm had tied her with. She was on the floor near the altar. "Kirsten, I'm here!"

He raised his sacrificial blade above his head. "Now, my Lords, I give you her black soul!"

The dagger turned white-hot in Simm's hands, searing his flesh to the bone. He screamed in agony and fell back from the altar.

The blade melted and splattered molten steel across the front of his black robe. The garment fell away in a flare of hell-fire.

Simm pulled his bleeding, destroyed hands apart, rubbing their remains over his charred face and hairless head. Naked and severely burned, he stumbled backward and rolled onto his right side facing toward the rim of the pit.

Thomas Farley wailed and moaned in the combined agony of all his victims.

"You're time is now, Tommy." The voice of Raven. Its deep, hollow sound rose from the depths of the hole. It whipped tendrils of rank vapor into a torrent.

Simm's agonized cries filled the chamber. "What have I done wrong?" He raised his head slowly. Blackened flesh tore open around his neck.

Raven's voice thundered from the pit. "You're a moron, Tommy. Not a single one of your victims had a black soul. They don't belong with us. Your offers were as useless as you are."

Simm's blistered eyelids fluttered. His lips cracked and bled as they moved. "Why did you stop me? Burn me?" The corners of his mouth tore open with the words.

Dense clouds of black oily smoke belched into the chamber. Something huge and reeking with putrid stench came out of the pit.

"Your burning has just begun, Tommy." The voice crashed against the walls vibrating support beams and cracking weak stones.

Tommy's baked-dry eyes saw the hideous

creature come out of the smoke and stand over him. His black swollen tongue split when he cried out, "I'm Simm, your servant!"

The beast bent forward, glaring through demonic, amber eyes. "I am Raven, the sixth demon. I am the keeper of the gate. "You are shit!"

Simm's lungs burned and drew no air. *I can't be alive*, he thought.

Raven read the mental scream. "You're not, Tom Farley. You are quite dead indeed."

Simm tried to squint. Both eyelids split and yellowish ooze ran like thick tears. He lifted his head abruptly. Charred flesh tore away from his right jawbone. His dead eyes focused on the unspeakable beast. *My offering … you—*

"You are the offering, you pathetic idiot." The creature laughed in a deep callous roar. "The gate's open, Tommy boy."

Simm turned away. Burned flesh tore from his right side. He gasped in agony and swallowed a chunk of his cooked tongue.

The demon bared its fangs and hissed an evil cry. Raven waved his huge right hand, seven, wailing black shadows rose out of the pit. "You are a source of amusement, Mr. Farley."

When Simm raised his arms cracked skin ripped from his ribs. He screamed in his mind, *I'm one of you!* Steaming, black blood gushed from Simm's ruined mouth and dripped onto his chest.

The beast glared through yellow-red eyes. "You're a joke to us, Mr. Farley—a filthy joke."

Raven and the seven shadows approached Simm's animated corpse. The beast thrust his right talons deep into Simm's burnt chest. He tore out the man's charred heart. "This is your gift, you stupid fool!" The organ burst into flame. The demon plunged it back into Simm's ravaged chest. "You've earned yourself a special place in hell, Tommy Farley." Raven turned to the seven shadows. "Take him."

Simm's remains were pulled down into the pit.

Raven went to the altar and carried Kirsten to where Anita lay. her clothes had been torn and she was bleeding from her mouth. He laid Kirsten beside her and studied the women with smoldering eyes.

"They have not earned a place in our kingdom yet." It was the demon of four heads and spoke in a deeper, ragged voice. "Send them back."

"Yes, my Lord." He waved his hand over the two women. "Be well. You'll remember nothing of this."

The painting of the four-headed beast exploded in flames and fell onto the crude altar setting it on fire.

Kirsten and Anita were gone.

The demons slipped into the pit and it closed up after them.

* * * *

Anita shut the hatch of her bright red 300-ZX. She grinned at Kristen. "What do you want to do tonight?"

"See a movie."

"Let's rent three horror flicks and gorge on buttered popcorn."

"It's a deal."

Anita looked back toward the festivities and drew a short breath.

"What is it?"

"I just felt a sudden chill."

They drove out of the parking lot in separate cars and left Oktoberfest behind for another year.

* * * *

The rage of the beast is in its breath of fire.

It holds the bleeding heart of innocence in the talons of its right hand. In the other it grips the grinning skull of death. The purpose of the beast is evil. Its goal is to feed the yawning mouth of Hell.

The Book of Dark Shadows

* * * *

The Fourth Demon

*P*aul Linderman drove his 56 Ford Crown Victoria out of Fort Bliss and headed toward town. There was a sleazy bar in El Paso where most of the soldiers hung out. The beer and the girls were cheap. Paul wanted a taste of both.

When he pulled into the parking lot an intense flash of lightning lit up the West Texas sky. A hard rain was on the way.

****

The brute at the door checked Paul's military ID and handed it back to him. "Have a ball, corporal."

"That's the idea."

An army buddy, Chuck Sayer, waved from a table near the dance floor. There were two girls with him Paul didn't recognize.

Chuck smiled and introduced the young women. "This lovely Latin flame is Carla. She's with me."

"For tonight, honey."

The blonde laughed, "He won't last an hour."

Chuck grinned. "Smart mouth there is, Sugar."

Paul shook her hand. "Sugar what?"

"Sugar is all you need to know, soldier. She took a sip of her screwdriver. "Can you make it for an hour?"

"I don't usually put a clock on it."

"With me you will, time is money, and my dance card is only open for short songs."

"You do have a smart mouth."

"It's yours whenever you're ready."

"I'll get back to you on that."

The waitress came to their table with a frosty mug of beer. "Hi, Paul, I brought your favorite."

"Thanks, Angie." He gave her a five. "Keep it."

"You're a peach."

Sugar pointed to her drink. "Buy me another, soldier?"

Paul nodded at the waitress and dug out a second five. "Keep that too." He smiled at Sugar. "I don't remember seeing you in this joint."

"I usually work the better clubs, but Carla thought slumming would be fun for a change."

"Bullshit, I did. It was you're idea and we ain't seen any green yet."

Chuck patted Carla's arm. "Hey, we're on for sure. Count on it."

"I'd better be counting it soon."

Sugar grinned at Paul, "What about you, soldier?"

"That depends on how much you charge for a dance." He studied Sugar's eyes. A flash of another young girl crossed his mind. "I may not be able to afford a date with someone from the better clubs."

"Shit." Carla looked across the room then turned away.

"Goddamn!" Sugar put her back to the entrance.

Paul and Chuck looked at the girls, then at each other.

To Carla, Chuck said, "What's wrong, sweet cakes?"

A lumbering civilian with an obtrusive gut and doorway-filling shoulders came up to their table and glared down at Sugar. He stood at least six-foot four, looked mean and smelled of sour sweat.

The man ignored Paul and Chuck. "Sugar," he grunted in a whisky-thick voice, "I got a hundred an' you're gonna fuck an' suck for it." He bumped the table, sloshing their drinks.

Paul grabbed his beer and said, "Easy, Pal, you're spilling my brew." He smiled up at the towering man.

The human hulk wiped sweat off his shaved head and looked down at Paul as he might regard a cockroach. He grinned, showing crooked, yellow teeth.

Paul saw the *beast* in the man's eyes.

The big man said, "Pack your army ass outta here, fuck-face, before I pop your Goddamn head like a puss-bump." He returned his attention to Sugar.

Paul stared at him. *That pig is the fourth demon.* He thought of the other three and gritted his teeth.

Carla looked up at the mass of drunken bulk. "Fuck off, Jake." She had fear in her voice. "We're busy."

"I'm not talkin' to you, spic-cunt. I'm talkin' to my sweet Sugar, the head-queen." He grabbed Chuck by the shirt and lifted him out of his chair. "What the fuck you lookin' at, puke-face?"

Paul sipped some beer. *The exact words of stinking, Billy Perkins who murdered my*

Allison. A chill like a column of fire ants skittered up Pauly's spine.

It's him, Paul! Allison's voice whispered from a corner of Paul's mind. *Get out of there— take Sugar with you.*

"I'm with Carla," said Chuck, trying to keep his balance.

The huge man swayed and smiled maniacally. He put his fat face close to Chuck's and spoke on a gust of rotten breath. "Take your little pecker and the Mexican-bitch away from me or I'll tear off your ugly face." Jake let the young man slide back into his chair and waited.

"Yes, sir." He wanted to get as far away from Jake as he could.

"Move, idiot–now!"

Chuck pushed himself from the table. He grabbed Carla by the arm and dragged her away.

Sugar said, "Jake, you're drunk. Let it go." She stared at the man-beast with tears in her eyes.

Paul sensed her pain. Something had happened before. This *pig* had hurt her.

Jake pushed against the table, spilling all the drinks but Paul's. He held it safely in his hand. Others, at nearby tables, gave the slob instant room. He took a handful of Sugar's hair and pulled her out of her seat. "You owe me a suck!" He growled, slapped a hundred on the wet table. "There's an extra twenty so I can do what you love best."

Paul jumped to his feet, threw the rest

of his beer in Jake's face, punched him in the mouth three times and kneed the animal in the groin. Jake bent forward, Paul slammed his beer mug against the back of the pig's head. He grabbed Sugar and pulled her through the crowd, out of the bar and into driving rain–sheets of hot, West Texas rain.

****

They drove toward a restaurant in a better section of town. On the way they talked about the bully Pauly had put down.

"What did that animal do to you?"

"He took a lot more than he paid for." The girl shuddered and pulled her wet jacket around her.

"Like what?"

"You want chapter and verse?" Sugar took a pack of cigarettes from her purse and lit one.

"I'm concerned. Is that a problem?" He glanced at her. The rain reflected patterns of colored lights across her face. "Jake scared the hell out of you the second he walked into that cesspool."

"Yeah." She took a deep drag on her cigarette and opened the wing window.

"Right. And he shook Carla pretty bad too, so what happened?" Paul eased the Vic through a flooded intersection.

"Look, it was a while back. He's a rotten bastard and I don't want to talk about it–okay?"

"No, not okay. Scumbags like Jake are not *people,* they're beasts!

"Tell me about it." Sugar moved closer to the passenger door.

"How much more will it cost?"

"For what?" She inhaled smoke and stared at him.

"For you to stop the crap, and accept a little friendliness. You're trying so hard to be a tough broad it's funny."

"Yeah?"

"Yeah. You're more than that, so cut the act."

She sucked another drag off her smoke. "Who the fuck are you, my big brother?"

"If I were, I'd kick your ass."

"I don't believe this. You're a fucking reformer."

Heavy rain hammered against the windshield faster than the wipers could clear it away. Paul pulled into the restaurant parking lot and stopped. "You just can't handle it, can you?"

"Handle what?"

"Somebody caring enough to be nice to you."

"I don't know from nice."

"Horse shit."

"Listen, Mr. Reformer, if you ain't gonna pay me and do it, then take me where I can get another trick." She flicked her cigarette butt through the open wing window.

"It's not that easy, sugar-baby!" He raised his fisted hand. "I own you tonight—what I say you do." He leaned forward and spoke through clenched teeth. "You're mine, bitch—whatever I want, you give. If you don't, I'll smash your pretty little face."

Sugar grabbed for the door handle.

"Please—I'll do whatever you want."

He held her arms. "You're all mine now."

She pressed against the door, turned pale and began shaking. Her eyes filled with tears. "I'll do anything you want. Don't hurt me …."

"That's what Jake did, isn't it?" Paul let go and gently touched her face.

She flinched and brought her hand up in self-defense. "Yes. The sonofabitch cut Carla's tits and busted my face!"

He winced and brushed strands of blonde hair away from her eyes. "I'm sorry … you don't have to tell me any more."

"Why did you scare me like that?"

"I needed to know … to be sure I was right. Jake is not a person."

"He's an animal, like you said. The pig. He broke my jaw and crushed my left cheekbone."

"Don't talk about it."

Sugar shifted her eyes to the colored reflections running across the windshield. "You wanted to hear it, so listen." She fumbled in her purse for her cigarettes. "The slob. After he finished beating and cutting, he tied us up and forced us to do everything three or four times … I don't remember exactly." She turned away and rolled down the passenger window a crack and cried.

The storm had moved on.

Paul brushed her hair again and smiled. To him, Sugar had become his long-lost love. He touched her tear-streaked cheek and remembered the bully's attack that killed his childhood girlfriend. He shivered as that dead December day crossed his mind. "Want some Mexican?"

"Huh?" She caught herself taking Pauly's hand and pressing it against her face.

"We're at a great Mexican place. How about having some chicken tacos with lots of sour cream and get a couple of big margaritas?"

"Yeah, sounds great …." She kissed him and leaned against the door smiling. In her heart, Sugar didn't feel like a whore right then. "Who are you, soldier?"

"I'm just a lonely corporal missing his sweetheart."

"You have one?"

"Not anymore." An image of Allison flashed across the back of his mind. "I had a girl once. A *beast* like Jake took her from me."

"She dumped you for a piece of shit like him?"

"A *monster* like that killed my girl."
"Oh, my God—how?"

"It was a long time ago. Allison was ice skating and he pushed her onto thin ice. She fell through and drowned."

"Did he ever get punished?"

"Not really, but he will be. I'm working on it."

"What?"

"The thing that killed Allison is evil and lives inside men like Jake. His time is up."

She laughed. "I sure thought it was when you whacked him with the beer mug."

"I didn't like the way he was talking to you and your girlfriend."

"Nobody goes after Jake. He'll be looking for you."

"Actually, I intend to find him and give the big lug a surprise apology."

"Don't try that. Jake'll hurt you bad and nobody will stop him.

"I'm not afraid of the evil in this world or the Jakes it possesses." He brushed her cheek with the back of his fingers. "Big Jake and I will have a nice chat. After that, you and Carla will never have to worry about him again."

"You know, Mr. Soldier … I think I like you a lot." Her eyes glistened in the colored lights from the restaurant. "I'm sorry for the way I talked in the bar. I want to be your Allison for the rest of the night."

"How much?"

"There's no charge for you."

He kissed her. For a moment, in the lights and shadows, Sugar became Allison again. She was only nine and smelled of summer flowers. He pulled back and looked at her. "Let's get some food and then I'll take you home where you'll be safe."

"Will you stay with me?"

"Not tonight. I have to have a word with Jake."

"You're serious?"

* * * *

Sugar finished her forth fish taco and took a sip from a second margarita and smiled. She studied Paul's face for a moment. "I said earlier I don't know from nice. I do now. You're the *nice* I've been missing all along."

"Thank you for saying so, I feel the same about you." He put his hand on hers. "There's a motel right next door and we're going over there when you finish your drink."

"Great, you've changed your mind."

"Yes, about taking you home."

"The motel would be just fine."

"You're checking in, alone."

"Why?"

"It's safer there."

"I'd rather be with you."

"We'll see each other again and I'll let

you be my girlfriend."

"I want to be that for you now. Jake won't come after me tonight. He doesn't know where we are."

"We're getting you checked in. I need to know you're okay while I tend to some business."

"You're really going back to the bar? Jake'll be long gone."

"I don't think so. Call Carla in the morning and have her pick you up or take a cab back to your place."

"How about you? I'm afraid of what you might get into."

"I'll be just fine." He waved at the waitress and pulled his wallet out of his uniform blouse. "Here's a hundred for you to cover the room and a good breakfast and a cab if you need one."

Sugar's eyes welled up. "You know how you make me feel?"

He smiled. "No, how?"

"Like a real person ... a woman worth something."

"You're all of that, Sugar, and more. Now, let's get you settled in."

* * * *

An hour later, Paul went into the bar through the back alley entrance. He stood in the shadowed hallway and looked out onto the dance floor. Jake was still there. Paul grinned and left.

1:45 AM:

He waited almost two hours in the shadows of the parking lot before Jake stumbled out of the gin mill and went to his pickup truck.

It's time, Paul.

Allison's voice crept out of a corner of his mind and pricked a sharp pain in his head.

He followed the truck to an isolated mobile home several miles outside of El Paso.

"I'll do it, Allison—this is the last killing."

The beast must die, my love. It's the only way you can set me free.

Paul walked up the rutted driveway and slipped his right hand into a tight black leather glove and pulled the eight inch hunting knife from its sheath.

A long time had passed since the last encounter with the beast. It seemed *unreal.*

Then he felt the unmistakable reality of the black dragon's hot, foul breath. The demon had returned and taken Jake's black heart, possessed it and filled it with untold evil. Jake had become *Billy-three* and therefore he must die.

Surprise was Paul's edge–his only edge. He pounded the butt of the knife on the door several times, and then flattened himself against the side of the trailer and waited.

What if he shoves a gun in my face? But he won't. I have the advantage. Maybe.

The trailer didn't have a porch. A few

concrete blocks served as steps, and that worked in Paul's favor.

Jake pushed the door open and let it slam against the side of the trailer opposite Paul's position. "Who the hell's bangin'?"

"Hey, *Puke-face!*

"Who the fuck are you?"

"I'm Paul Linderman. Remember Allison Rogers?"

The big man reached for him a bit too slow.

"Go back to hell where you belong." The blade sliced through Jake's groin in a swift upward motion and on to the center of the beast's chest. Hot blood gushed and splashed over Paul's hand. Jake gagged in horror and slipped down in the doorway. The knife cut across his left cheek. "That's for Sugar and Carla, you filthy pig."

Jake rolled into the small kitchen and bled all over the dirty white tile floor. He twitched and then went still. Paul stood over the body and steadied himself against the counter. Jake turned his head, and his face became Billy's face. It looked up and grinned. *"Fuck you, Linderman. Allison sucks cocks in hell!"* The illusion faded, becoming Jake again. The slob was dead.

Something vile and evil rose from Jake's body, flew out of the trailer and screamed, *"She's burning in hell!"*

Paul jerked away from the counter. His raincoat and shirt spattered with blood and foul.

"Jesus." In the mad frenzy of the attack, he'd lost his senses, but now he saw the violence. His stomach turned over and he retched. Vomit burned the back of his throat.

Night sounds rushed in through the open door, as though they might see and bear witness against him. He stepped over Jake's body, grabbed a dishtowel off a nearby rack, used it to turn on a faucet over the sink, and then washed the blood from his glove and the knife.

He used another wet towel to clean the blood from his raincoat, but the uniform shirt was hopeless. He would have to destroy it, along with the towels.

He rolled the body on its side and pulled Jake's wallet from the pants hip pocket. *Make it look like a robbery.*

The kitchen was a mess, but if Jake had startled a thief, there should have been a struggle with things broken, disarray, chaos … *Smash some things. Do it!*

When he finished, Jake's trailer resembled a disaster area. It was done. Billy was dead for good.

* * * *

On the way back to Fort Bliss, the encounter with Jake seemed like a distant nightmare, but what happened at the bar and the time spent with Sugar was still vivid.

Have I killed Billy again?

A dull pain crept in behind his eyes. He whispered Allison's name several times. "Tell me it's over." She did not respond. The migraine pulsed and dug deep into the corners of his brain, but still, Allison's voice did not come. One more *Billy-thing* lay dead in a trashed trailer.

"It has to be the last."

Lightning shattered the horizon ... four seconds ... thunder exploded.

The West Texas storm had returned to play out another act.

* * * *

The beast rides a pale horse
with the fury of hell
trailing behind.
It will find the weak of heart.
The demon lusts for the soul
of guilt.
Beware the rider of the pale
horse.

The Book of Dark Shadows

* * * *

Bobby has a Nightmare

*H*is sick headache had started right after supper and by seven, Bobby was in bed with all the lights out. His mother gave him two aspirin, but they didn't help in the least.

Janice opened the door part way and whispered, "I'll be in the living room if you need anything."

From under the pillow, where he had buried his head, Bobby answered, "Okay." The vibration of his own voice made his brain hurt. He'd suffered a few headaches in the past but none like this one. "Please, God," he prayed, "let me go to sleep … please."

The sandman began his work. It may have been Divine intervention, rather than medication. That didn't matter. Wonderful waves of drifting away eased the thud-thud, thud-thud in Bobby's skull.

He felt himself floating down, and a pinprick of light appeared at the center of an oily blackness. With it came mixed sounds of churning water and sloughing, winter wind. Singing wind, Grandpa called it. The wind that delivered storms and carried haunting voices under the eaves. The wind that rattles your bedroom windows in the dead of night just to let you know it was there.

The speck of light spun clockwise and filled the whole of Bobby's dream-vision. He slipped over the edge of consciousness and into the worst nightmare of his childhood.

Blood! Mamma–there's blood! His terrified scream was soundless. He thought the words. He felt them crawling in his throat, but he couldn't speak them.

Carol stood in the center of a pool of dark aortal blood. She was naked and touching herself, laughing. Her face was twisted into a chalk-white death mask.

Carol!

When Bobby opened his mouth to shout her name, squirming, black worms gushed out and splashed into the sickening gore. He clasped his hand over his mouth as an acid sting of vomit backed up in his throat. He choked and wrenched forward falling to his knees.

The girl and the blood vanished.

Bobby was on the hard floor of the garage feeling one of Judy's severed legs. His sister's limb was in a black stocking. A white patent leather shoe was buckled onto the foot. He jumped back screaming in silent horror. He was crying, unable to move.

Jane, Bobby's lost love appeared in winter clothes covered with fragments of frozen blood. "Albert's come back! Her voice echoed. Look what he's doing!" She pointed to the tattered couch and disappeared.

Albert was hunched over Carol and Judy. A broken piece of his spine protruded from his back. His head was twisted around toward Bobby. The right half of Albert's face had rotted away. The hideous Albert-thing laughed maniacally and finished chopping off Judy's other leg. It threw the bloody leg at Bobby and began stabbing Carol.

Both girls were bound and gagged. Their cries muffled, lost in the Albert-thing's demonic laughter. It soaked its hands in the blood of the victims and began rubbing Carol's legs.

Bobby dragged himself to the workbench, which was covered with large black spiders. He pulled open a drawer and his hunting knife was still there. "You puke!"

"Kill him, Bobby–kill him again!" Jane reappeared. Her Southern Belle dress stained with blood and black filth.

The thing rubbed more blood on Carol's legs and thighs. It laughed and bit into her stomach.

Bobby crawled toward the living-dead beast. The distance between them seemed to get wider. He forced himself forward. He was getting closer.

Judy screamed. "My legs! Bobby, He cut off my beautiful Legs!" She was no longer gagged.

Carol became Jane. She was dead. Her eyes had turned milk-white. Her small mouth was gushing filthy water. Her blonde curls hung in strands of slime and dark mud.

Bobby pushed forward through thick black liquid.

The snarling Albert-thing grunted and vomited foul worms and yellow bile in his face. He shook his head and yelled, "You stinking, filthy garbage!" The hunting knife sunk into Albert's broken neck all the way to the handle. Again and again, Bobby plunged the blade deep into every part of the beast he could. He hacked at the abomination. Chunks of flesh fell away. The thing morphed into a serpent with a long black forked tongue and red eyes.

Albert became the beast in the story that Bobby and Jane shared one day in school. He knew what must be done. He gripped his knife, which had turned into a sword and brought it down on the neck of the demon. The steel broadsword cut off the head of the serpent with a sharp *ringing sound,* which echoed off the walls of the garage. It became a shadowy damp cave deep inside a coal-black mountain.

No Albert-thing. No dragon. Nothing. "Jane!" he screamed, his voice echoing. He ran headlong into thick blackness and stopped. A keening sound, rising and falling, came from the inky void. The darkness was like no other he had experienced. It was heavy and filled with threat. It was a living thing that pressed around him, seeking with its cold black hands.

Bobby whimpered. The keening and moaning stopped.

Silence.

Strands of gray light appeared in the distance. His legs were rubbery–numb. When he reached the source of light he found himself outside in an endless cemetery.

Wailing, bitter wind swept through the leafless limbs of black deformed trees. Snow covered ground was spattered with steaming blood. The headstones were identical, and each bore the epitaph, *JANE ROGERS: MURDERED BY ALBERT PERKINS.*

* * * *

Bobby sat straight up in bed covered with a sheen of cold sweat. A scream of Jane's name was trapped in his throat.

The migraine was gone. All the pounding pain had found its way into his heart.

Jane's voice whispered through his head. *It was just a bad dream. Albert is not dead. He will come back. Set me free, Bobby ... you have to kill him again.*

Shadows of the nightmare faded, but for Bobby the nightmare had just begun.

* * * *

Dreams are echoes from the soul.
They wait in deep corners of the mind.

The Book of Dark Shadows

The Last Waltz

*H*arold Parish prepared to cry, again.

He pressed play on the remote and started the DVD for what must have been the five-hundredth time.

"I love you, Ruth," he whispered.

The scene started, music filled the living room. Harold felt the sting of tears once more.

The dance was their first as husband and wife and it was thirty-five years old. Harold had the Super-Eight film transferred to DVD two-years ago, just one month before Ruth had passed away.

He pressed slow-motion on the remote and wiped his eyes. He wanted to enjoy reading Ruth's lips form the words, *I'll love you forever.* The grief forced his chest to heave.

Between sobs He spoke to the screen, "I will always be here for you and I will always care for you."

Unfortunately, Harold could not stop the disease that ate the life out of Ruth's heart.

In the darkened room the dancing images seemed to come to life. Harold could feel Ruth's arms around him and enjoy the scent of her perfume.

"I miss you so much my love ... I pray that you can hear me."

He stood and pretended to hold his wife and dance with her one more time.

Just two days before, on the second anniversary or her death, Harold had brought another bouquet of tea roses to her grave. He knelt before her headstone and touched it with his gentle hand.

"My life is so empty without you. I've watched our first dance so many times I'm wearing out the disc." The words caught in his throat. "You were so beautiful and you made me the happiest man alive." Sobs came, as they always had on every visit to Ruth's grave.

Harold replaced the old flowers with the fresh roses. "I would give my soul just to dance with you one more time."

* * * *

Two days later, Harold finished his imaginary dance with his departed wife. He hit pause on the remote and froze the frame and studied the image. "I can't go on anymore, Ruth. There is no life without you."

The DVD started playing on its own and Harold heard Ruth's words this time. "I'll love you forever."

"What?"

The scene played again. "I'll love you forever."

A weak knock sounded on the front door.

"Who is it?" Harold glanced at the large TV screen. The dance scene played again.

Another soft knock.

He went to the door and opened it. A wave of decay drifted in on the night air. The odor of damp earth came with it.

"I've come back, my love." Ruth smiled through what was left of her face. Her eyes were gone. Deep inside the empty sockets a flame of life flickered. She held out her skeletal arms. Pieces of her funeral gown fell away. She stepped into the foyer. "Shall we dance?"

Harold led Ruth into the living room and started the DVD. "I've missed you so much."

Music filled the room.

Harold and Ruth embraced and danced their last waltz.

* * * *

Mr. Bailey & Mr. Brown

SCHENECTADY, NY – FEBRUARY 2010:

*A*nother freezing morning and more snow predicted.

"Excuse me." Jonathan squeezed by a fellow passenger and went to the front of the bus.

"Right on time, Mr. Bailey."

"Thank you George, you're a good man."

"That's what my wife says." The driver laughed and opened the door. "You have a good day."

"They're all the same anymore." He trudged through the small mound of dirty snow in front of Carl's Pawn and Loan. The sidewalk was icy. Mr. Bailey shuffled along to the door beside the pawn shop. He set his briefcase down and dug the keys out of his coat pocket. He brushed snow off the shingle on the door. Jonathan Bailey – CPA & Notary.

He felt the warm rub of the Russian-Gray against his leg. "No, Chester. You can't come up. You know Mr. Brown is allergic to cats." He reached down and scratched Chester's ears. "Paul opens in an hour. He'll feed you like he does every day." Jonathan unlocked the door and managed to get into the hallway before the cat could.

One flight up to the office. Every day the stairs seemed to gain more steps. At sixty-two, Mr. Bailey took longer to climb them.

When he got inside, Jonathan pulled off his overshoes, hung up his coat, hat and scarf and turned up the heat. It wouldn't take long to get the cramped office warmer.

"Mr. Brown, I'm in."

He went to the tiny kitchenette to make coffee when the phone rang. "Not even eight and they're calling." He stepped back to his desk and answered the phone. "Jonathan Bailey, CPA."

"Good morning Jon, Ken James here."

"Yes, sir?" He noticed Mr. Brown and nodded.

"Listen, I'm sorry to call so early, but I need a favor." Kenneth James had been a client for twenty years.

"It's Bobby again, I suspect." He grinned at Mr. Brown and shook his head. "What's your number one son gotten into now?" He carried the handset back to the counter and opened the can of Yuban dark roast.

"Bobby filed early and has caught an audit."

"It's not the end of the world. I'm open Wednesday after lunch. Have him bring all his papers and I'll see what I can do."

"I appreciate it, Jon."

"You're welcome, Ken. Have a good day." He glanced over at Mr. Brown. "Why do we always say that?"

The old iron radiators popped and groaned while Jonathan went about fixing his pot of coffee. "I take it your weekend went well."

Mr. Brown didn't comment.

"Mine was the same old, same old." He put cream and sugar into his cup and waited for the brewer to finish. "Sometimes I wish there were no weekends." He opened an old fashioned breadbox and took out a loaf of fresh cheese bread. "Back in the day, before my wife passed, Saturdays and Sundays were special." Jonathan cut two thick slices and put them in the microwave for a few seconds. "We went to dinner, dancing and movies.

What a great time we had." He removed the bread from the oven, and took them to his desk with his cup of coffee. "As they say, those were the days." Jonathan pulled apart pieces of one warm slice and set them in front of Mr. Brown. "Now I have you to share with."

For a mouse, Mr. Brown was quite large and handsome. He had a rich coat and healthy, shiny black eyes and never did his business on Jonathan's desk. He had been a good friend for more than a year. Mr. Brown sat up on his haunches and nibbled on a large chunk of cheese bread. *You know, Jonathan, it's time you made a change.*

Mr. Bailey took a sip of coffee. "Yeah, I suppose you're right—what!" He sat back, spilled some coffee and stared at the mouse.

Don't be alarmed. I'm speaking in your head.

"You're speaking?"

No, not actually speaking. I can't. Boy, have I tried. I wanted to talk to you for a year, but my mouth won't let me form words. Every time I try it comes out as a squeak."

Jonathan pushed away from his desk. "I'm losing it."

You're okay, Jonathan, relax. May I call you Jon? It's hard enough with this telepathy thing without trying to use long names."

"Call me Jon?" He shook his head and

rubbed his eyes. Mr. Brown was still there munching on a piece of bread. "I was afraid of a breakdown like this."

There's no breakdown, you're fine. We need to talk, okay?

"I'm having a conversation with a mouse." Jonathan gulped some coffee.

Yeah, I think it's great. Would you excuse me for a few minutes?

"Okay, sure … whatever."

This cheese bread is excellent. I want to take some to the kids."

"To the kids? Yeah go ahead."

Mr. Brown picked up a large chunk of bread and scurried off.

The phone rang.

"Jonathan Bailey, CPA."

"Hi, it's Rachel Norman. I want to file early this year. Can I get in before the rush?"

"That's a good idea. Sure. I think Thursday would be fine. How about one PM?"

"That's perfect. See you then."

"Excellent, bye." Jonathan studied the pieces of cheese bread on his desk. "This isn't real."

Mr. Brown popped up on the desk and took another piece of bread in his front paws and chewed a few nibbles. *The kids love the bread and the wife says she'd like to make you a casserole, but we mice can't do things like that.*

"I don't imagine you can."

Jon, you have to consider moving on. Your life's been hell for the last year. Now you're wishing there weren't any weekends. I felt your pain when your wife died. It's time.

"I have a business here." He pulled up to his desk and held out another piece of bread to Mr. Brown. The mouse took it in his front paws. "What would I do? Where would I go?"

Get real, think. There's a train out of here every day headed west. Buy a ticket. Go to California, hang your shingle on a door in Hollywood. Do accounting for the stars, make a fortune and live like they do. You owe it to yourself. Besides, it's a nice long relaxing trip by train.

Jonathan sat back and studied the mouse. "How can I possibly do it, Mr. Brown? I have obligations here."

Sell the business and the house and just go. The mouse took another piece of cheese bread from Jonathan's fingers. *Just do it.*

"What about you and the family?" He fed the mouse another piece of bread.

We'll survive, we always do.

"You've been a good friend." He scratched Mr. Brown's ears.

So have you. Go do it, and don't look back. He grabbed a chunk of bread and ran off.

* * * *

Two months later, Mr. Bailey sat in the club car of a westbound train enjoying a cocktail. The porter approached. "Can I get you anything else, sir?"

"Are there any mice on this train?"

"I hardly think so."

Jonathan smiled. "Well, there should be." He raised his glass. "To you and your family, Mr. Brown."

* * * *

Author Notes

J hope you enjoyed my crazy story. Believe it or not, part of this tale is true.

In 1974 I was going through a bad time. I was working three jobs at the time. I worked for a San Diego radio station on the full-time overnight shift. I was paid $400 a month. One hundred of that was going for rent at a crummy motel. I drove cab from 5:00 to 11:00 PM Monday through Friday. My third job was working in the darkroom at a camera store developing film and printing pictures for other people. In total I made about $600 a month.

I lived on oatmeal, cheese and crackers and canned stew.

I slept between jobs. I wrote when I could on a manual typewriter and used a lot of White-Out to cover my errors.

Saturday night was my time off. One Saturday night, I lay in bed reading. I caught movement out of the corner of my eye. I had dropped a piece of saltine cracker on the floor. A mouse had found it. He took it and scampered back into the cupboard through the badly-fitted doors.

I began feeding the little creature every day. Within a few weeks he was eating out of my hand. He would take hold of my fingers and nibble away at the bread or cracker I was offering. He would often take what I gave him and scamper away. He had a family way back in the cupboard and took the food to feed them.

The mouse never spoke to me, but I talked to him. He was a friend. I named him, Mr. Brown.

I raise a glass to Mr. Brown every time I remember him. He was a good friend.

Ted

Ellen Takes a Stand

*E*llen Morgan helped the delivery guy in with the bags of groceries. "You're late, Phillip."

"I'm sorry, ma'am. It's Friday and the market was swamped." The young man put two bags on the kitchen table and grinned. "I made sure I got the best New York steak for you."

"I didn't mean to snap at you. My husband's due home in less than an hour." A familiar chill worked its way up her arms. The goose bumps weren't visible through the sleeves of her blouse. She made sure the bruises were hidden. The marks on her face weren't as easy to hide.

She took her purse off the sparkling clean counter and gave the lad a five-dollar tip. "How much for the groceries?"

"Eighty six seventy-five and ten for the delivery."

Ellen wrote him a check and smiled. The cut on her upper lip stung. "I'm sorry, I didn't mean to bark at you."

"It's okay. I'm the one who was late." He hesitated. "Mrs. Morgan?"

"Yes?"

"Are you sure you're okay?"

"I'm fine. Thank you for your help." She walked him to the front door. "Thank you for caring."

"You're welcome."

* * * *

Twenty minutes later Ellen had prepared the mixture for the scrambled eggs that would go with Bert's New York steak. She seasoned the meat precisely as he demanded and put the cut in the fridge. *I said I'm sorry twice to a young man I hardly know.* She shook her head and set the table.

* * * *

At the sound of garage door opening Ellen glanced at the kitchen clock. Six on the dot.

The all too familiar rumble of Bert's expensive red Mustang sent a razor-sharp sting up the back of her neck. *He's home.*

Bert came into the kitchen. "Any calls?"

"Your secretary left a message on the machine in your office. It's something about Paul Harper canceling his appointment for tomorrow morning."

"Why didn't you call my cell and let me know?"

"I thought you'd check your messages. I'm sorry."

"Thought?" He loosened his tie. "The day you start thinking hell will freeze over."

"I'm sorry, honey."

"You're always sorry about something."

His words cut deeper than usual. *Don't say sorry again!* She drew in a slow breath. "I'm fixing your favorite dinner. New York steak just the way you like it with snow peas, whipped mashed potatoes and scrambled eggs on the side. I used chicken broth instead of water on the spuds."

"Sounds great. Let's see if you get it right. That would be a wonder."

"You'll love it. I'll open a bottle of Merlot."

"I guess you can't screw that part up much." Bert laughed. "Have it on the table in fifteen minutes." He went to his home office.

* * * *

Ellen took a small bite of steak and grinned at her husband. "Is it okay?"

Bert sipped some wine and stared at his wife. "This is what you call a good steak dinner?"

"What's wrong?" Shards of imaginary glass shot through Ellen's heart and brought tears to her eyes. "I fixed it the way you like."

"Watery potatoes and over cooked meat doesn't cut it!" He got up from the table, picked up his plate and scraped the food into the garbage. "What the hell good are you?" He went to Ellen and backhanded her across the face. "You can't handle a simple message from my office and then you screw up a dinner!"

"I'm sorry."

"Yes you are, you always are." He hit her again.

She lost her balance and fell against the refrigerator. She grabbed for the counter to keep from going to the floor and knocked the checkbook into the sink. "Don't hit me any more."

"What did you say?" He stepped closer.

"I said, don't hit me—don't ever hit me again!" She glared at the man and didn't move.

Bert chuckled and took the checkbook out of the sink. He saw the grocery receipt and picked it up. His eyes flashed with anger. "You lazy bitch!" The slap of the leather checkbook across Ellen's face echoed off every appliance in their chef's kitchen. "You can't take your fat ass to the store?" The second blow glanced off her right arm. "Is there something wrong with the BMW?"

"I wanted to have more time to fix your dinner."

"Well, you screwed that up and spent ten bucks for delivery." He raised his hand.

"Don't do it, Bert. Just don't."

He tossed the checkbook on the center island and grinned. "I'm hearing a lot of smart-mouth out of you lately."

"I'm tired of your meanness and it's getting worse." She started clearing the table. "Is there trouble at work? You're coming home angrier every day ... I care about you ... we could talk, I'll listen."

He picked up his glass. "If I did have a problem at the office you wouldn't understand it anyway. Why waste my breath discussing it with you?"

"Maybe sharing could curb some of your temper."

He took a sip of wine and stared at his wife. "Have you been having heart-to-heart sessions with your sister again?"

Ellen scraped some of the wasted food into the compactor. "I don't visit Joan much anymore. We talk on the phone. She's not buying into my made up excuses for black eyes and wearing long sleeve blouses in August." She slammed drawer shut and pressed the start button. "That's why I have the groceries delivered. I'm embarrassed by the looks I get at the super market."

He laughed at her. "They probably wonder why you waddle like a duck these days."

"You've become a cruel man … you're not the Bert Morgan I married."

"Look in the mirror, Ellen. You're not the lovely little thing that took my heart."

"Actually, my dear, I don't think you ever really had one."

"That's enough of your sass for one evening." He finished his wine and poured another. "I'm having people from the office over on Sunday."

"That's nice. Thanks for letting me know. What am I supposed to do about feeding them?"

"I wouldn't let you screw that up. I'm having it catered."

"And you got mad over a ten dollar delivery charge?"

"Enough backtalk. You're starting to forget your place around here." He picked up the bottle of Merlot and smiled. "When you finish cleaning up the kitchen get to work on the patio."

"You don't have an appointment in the morning. You clean it."

Bert's face stiffened and his gray eyes turned cold. He set the bottle and glass on the island. "You have pissed me off, woman."

Two steps and he was on her. The first

smack across her mouth opened the sore on her upper lip. The second made a fresh cut. Ellen spit blood on his forty-dollar custom tailored powder blue shirt. "That's it you bastard!" she pushed him back and spit again. "I hope you got a thrill out that. It's the last time you'll ever hit me! Try it once more and you'll wish to god you were never born!"

"Don't press your luck." He pinched her nose. "Hey, there are no tears."

"I have none left." The copper taste of blood filled her mouth. Ellen swallowed hard. *I will not cry.* She said it again in a whisper, "I will not cry."

Bert went back to the island and picked up the wine bottle and glass. "I'm going to change my shirt and do some work in my office. I'll be listening for the sounds of you cleaning up the patio."

"I might do that, then again, I may not."

"Oh, I think you will."

SATURDAY MORNING – 7:30:

Ellen brushed her auburn hair for the third time and studied her image in the bathroom mirror. "I look like I fell off a coaster at Disneyland." She pasted more cover up on her bruised right cheek bone. "Who are you trying to kid?"

Another layer of red lipstick didn't make much difference. "Shit." She went to the kitchen and called her sister.

* * * *

Joan picked up on the third ring. "Ellen? How nice. I haven't heard from you in two months. Glad to know you're still among the living."

"I have to see you. Can I come over?"

"Of course. Are you all right?"

"I am now. Is Frank there?"

"He's doing golf at the country club."

"I'll be there in fifteen minutes."

"You sound funny. Is something wrong?"

"Not anymore. I'm on the way."

* * * *

Joan set two cups and saucers on the dining room table and went back to the kitchen for the coffee service and a plate of French pastries. Ellen tapped on the side door. "It's open, Sis."

The younger woman stepped in and closed the door. "The gate guard looked at me twice before he let me in."

Joan turned away from the counter and almost dropped the plate. "My good God in heaven!"

"Nice huh?"

"Bert did that?"

"Who else? I don't usually get into bar fights or bang my face against the wall."

"That sonofabitch!"

"Worse actually. I shook all the way over here. I need to sit down."

"In the other room, I made coffee."

Ellen put her purse on the kitchen table and followed her sister into the elegant formal dining room. "He did most of this damage last night. Some of it's left over from a week ago."

"You need medical attention right now. It's no wonder the guard didn't recognize you. I wouldn't have either." She poured coffee for both of them. "Your upper lip is twice its size and your whole face is swollen."

"Would Frank help me get a lawyer?" She took a careful sip of coffee.

"He certainly will. We talked about your situation before, but Frank made it clear that you have to press charges."

"Your husband is the best there is, but he's a corporate attorney. That won't work in this case."

"Of course not. Frank's playing golf this morning with three civil attorneys. One of them is Jim Wallace. He'd take your case in a heartbeat. He's one of the best in the city."

"Joan." Ellen fought her tears. "I need a criminal lawyer."

"Fantastic! You're going to drag that man into court and let the world see what the famous Bert Morgan is really all about. I can hear the news reports. Well known Century Electronics CEO, B. K. Morgan found guilty of assault and battery in his wife beating trial. I love it! You're finally doing the right thing." She patted her sister's hand. "Good for you, Ellen. Frank will get Jim to represent you and we'll testify on your behalf. We wanted you do this three years ago."

Ellen blotted her swollen eyes and took another careful sip of coffee. "I tried to warn him. I even made a couple of threats. He just grinned or laughed or both."

"I'm proud of you. Frank and I will help with legal expenses. You can stay here until you get the house. You will win this, but you know Bert will fight and he'll make bail on the charges." Joan clapped her hands and ate a bite of pastry. "Damn, this is good news."

"When Bert hit me the last time he opened a new cut on my lip." She touched the sensitive spot under her thick lipstick. "I knew it had to be now or never."

"Weren't you afraid of what he'd do when you told him?"

"I didn't say anything right then. I had to work it all out in my head first."

"That was probably wise."

"Will you and Frank stand by me through

this no matter what?"

"I've already made that clear. There is no question." She poured fresh coffee for her sister and herself. "How did you approach him with the news?"

"I remember every detail and every word I said." Ellen put a small piece of pastry in her aching mouth. The sting covered the sweetness of the confection. "I crawled in bed next to Bert."

"You're sleeping with that bastard?"

"If I try staying in the guest room he drags me out and beats me again."

"This is insane. We'll take everything he's got."

"I couldn't sleep and I was sick thinking about what I was going to have to face." She winced when she sipped some coffee. "I got out of bed in the middle of the night." Ellen shook her head and shuddered.

Everything came rushing back.

* * * *

THE SAME DAY – 3:00 AM:

Ellen pushed back the covers and sat on the edge of the bed. She looked over at the sleeping man. *Eight years with you.* The thought sent a sharp pain through her heart.

A moment later she sat at Bert's huge oak desk and reached for the power switch on his computer. *What are you going to do, send him an email?*

The gold-framed picture of her and Bert from a happier time caught her eye. Tears welled up. *No, girl. You will not write a note. You will not cry.* She touched the photograph and whispered, "You're going to face him and bring hell to an end."

* * * *

She turned on all the lights in the bedroom and poked Bert's leg. "Wake up." Ellen jabbed at him again and raised her voice, "I said, wake up!" Her heart pounded in her ears. Adrenalin rushed through her body.

Bert turned over and sat up, half awake. When he saw the gun, he came fully alert. "Jesus-god, what the hell are you doing!"

"Something I should've done years ago." Ellen jacked a shell into the chamber of the twelve gauge. "Don't get out of bed. Sit back and listen to me."

"You stupid bitch!" He started to get up.

The shotgun blast filled the room. A hole the size of a baseball appeared in the cherry wood headboard just inches from where Bert's head would've been. "Didn't I just tell you to listen?"

"You're dumber than I thought. Give me that gun!"

"Apparently the shot affected your hearing." The second explosion shattered the bed lamp and Bert's clock radio and made a larger hole in the wall. "That's two. There are five more itching to get out."

"Are you crazy?" He started to get to his feet.

"Stand up and I'll blow your legs off!" She pumped another round into the gun. "You've made me go nuts. Eight years, Bert—seven of them have been a nightmare. Where did I go wrong?" She started to shake. "I loved you ... we loved each other once ... where did all that go?"

"I'm sorry, honey." He stood.

The third blast destroyed Bert's right knee. He fell back on the bed in agony.

"Sorry?" She jacked another shell into the Browning. "Still don't think I mean business? There are four left now and guess what, you're going to get them."

"Please, Ellen ... it's not too late. Call 911. I'll never hit you again, I promise. I'm bleeding to death!" He tried to wrap his wound in the blankets and writhed in pain. "Please—dear God ... you're killing me."

"I guess I intended to do that." She pointed the barrel at his face. "Guess what really did it for me."

"Ellen, for god's sake help me."

She wiped sweat off her brow. "Your last comment before you went to your office." Ellen stepped closer. "Just the way you said it was the last straw." She leaned down close to her husband's sweating contorted face. "Don't be here Sunday when my people come over. I don't want my associates to see how you look."

"I'm so sorry … I was upset. Please … call 911—I can't stand this pain."

"Look at me, Bert—look at my face—look at it!" She leaned closer. "You did this you bastard! You mean son-of-a-bitch!"

The remaining rounds exploded Bert's head and chest. She dropped the shotgun and fell to her knees on the bedroom floor. "What have I done … dear God, what have I done?" All of her frustration and anger drained out of her.

The smell of cordite filled the silent room.

A neighbor's dog barked in the distance.

* * * *

JOAN'S DINING ROOM – PRESENT TIME:

Ellen started to cry. "When it was done there was blood all over the wall. I didn't really feel much of anything except I knew full well that I had murdered my husband."

Joan choked and sat stiff. "Are you aware

of what will happen?"

"Of course she is." Frank stepped in from the kitchen. "I was listening. Can you think clearly?"

"I guess I can."

"Did the shotgun belong to Bert?"

"No, I bought it three weeks ago."

"That's not good."

Joan said, "What's wrong with that?"

"It's evidence of premeditation. That is an open charge of murder in the first degree. The DA's office will get an indictment in a heartbeat."

Ellen looked at Frank. "I did plan to kill him."

"You're facing twenty-five to life or the death penalty."

"I did it. There's no doubt about that."

Joan drew a short breath. "We have to do something. That bastard had it coming."

"A jury has to make that decision and they may not agree."

Ellen dabbed her eyes. "I've created a major mess, Sis … I'm so sorry."

Joan grabbed her sister's hands. "Don't say that. Never again are you to be sorry for blowing that shit into kingdom come."

Frank punched a number into his cell phone. "Hi, Jason. Glad I caught you at home. Hang on." He turned to the two women. "I need to take this in my office."

Ellen blotted her eyes. "I'm going to jail."

Joan nodded. "From what I know of the law, there's a good chance you will."

"I'll die there."

"No—no you won't. We're going to help, I promise."

"I knew this would happen. All the agony I've been through and now I've brought more on myself."

* * * *

Frank returned to the dining room. "Jason Parish will take your case. He's the best criminal defense attorney in the state. He sat beside her and held her shaking hand. "Right now we need to face reality." He looked at his wife. "Can we have some more coffee? She's going to need it."

"What have I done to my family?" Ellen shook her head and fought more tears. "I just killed a man."

"Don't say that again from now on. Jason will be here in about a half hour and he will coach you on all the details."

"I'm completely lost. I'm in limbo." She gripped Frank's hand. "I blew Bert's head off. I've never seen so much blood in my life. I married that man, I made love to him—I *was* in love with him."

"I understand. Put it behind you as best you can."

"I'm frightened. I'll go to jail." She shook.

"That crossed my mind, but now it's a reality."

"You committed a capital crime and it was premeditated." He patted her hand again. "I can tell you this much. A strong part of Jason's defense will be long term mental and physical abuse. Unfortunately, your face will heal before you go to trial. The first priority is to get all your makeup off immediately and then let me take some digital pictures of your face. Joan can get shots of any other bruises."

"What's going to happen now?"

"Jason has notified the police and your house will soon become a crime scene. Some time in the next hour two homicide detectives will be here to arrest you for murder."

"I'm so sorry, Frank … so sorry."

"They will read you your rights and take you into custody. You say nothing to them. I mean nothing! When Jason gets here, he'll tell you more."

"Can't I stay here?"

"I'm afraid not." He squeezed her hand. "You'll be held until Monday. Jason will be with you at the arraignment."

"Am I going to be interrogated?"

"I doubt that. You're not denying the crime. After you plead not guilty, the assistant DA will ask the judge for remand."

"But I killed Bert." She started to cry.

"Your plea has to be not guilty or there will

be no trial. Jason will explain everything."

"I'll live with this nightmare for the rest of my life."

"The ADA will want to put you in jail until the trial."

"I'd never survive."

"Chances are, that isn't going to happen. You're not a flight risk; you have no prior criminal record. Jason will request bail and you'll stay with us until after the trial."

"Thank you … thank you both."

"Ellen, do you really understand the gravity of the charges that will be brought against you?"

"I murdered my husband."

"You planned the killing and that makes it tougher for Jason's defense."

"I didn't really want to do it."

"That doesn't matter. You shot Bert several times. That will make a difference with the jury. If Jason can get the charge reduced to second degree manslaughter, you'll have a better chance at beating this."

* * * *

Joan sat beside her sister and hugged her. "No matter what, Jason, Frank and I are going to get you through all of it."

Frank led Jason and two detectives into the

living room. Jason said, "These men are detectives Chambers and Berris from the San Diego Police Department."

Berris did the honors. "Mrs. Ellen Morgan, would you please stand and put your hands behind your back."

She hugged Joan once more and stood.

The detective continued, "Mrs. Morgan, you're under arrest for the murder of Bert Morgan. You have the right to remain silent. Anything you say can and will be used against you in a court of law. If you can't afford an attorney, one will be appointed for you. Do you understand these rights?"

"Yes." When the cuffs closed on her wrists, Ellen began to sob.

* * * *

THREE MONTHS LATER:
SAN DIEGO COUNTY SUPERIOR COURT:
DEPARTMENT #4
JUDGE JULIE ANDERSON PRESIDING:

The courtroom was packed with Bert's friends and associates. Both side aisles were lined with members of the media.

Silence.

Judge Anderson addressed the ADA. "Is the prosecution ready with its summation?"

"We are your honor."

"Proceed."

Assistant District Attorney Amanda Cornwell approached the jury of seven women and five men. Four of the jurors were not married.

"All through the days and weeks of this grueling trial you've been asked, by the defense, to believe that Ellen Morgan acted out of mortal fear for her life." She pointed to the defendant. "Mrs. Morgan shot her husband while he lay in his bed. She pumped five rounds of double-ought buckshot blasts into a defenseless man."

She paced in front of the judicial panel and shook her head slowly for affect. "The prosecution has clearly proven that the victim did not own a firearm of any kind. The defendant purchased the murder weapon three weeks before the killing. That, ladies and gentlemen, is pure criminal intent. Not once in eight years of marriage did Ellen Morgan call 911 to report spousal abuse. Mr. Bert Morgan was a pillar in the business community of this great city. He was respected by his associates and employees. He never had so much as a parking ticket."

Amanda paced again and scanned the jurors. "It is your duty to find Ellen Morgan guilty of murder in the first degree." She returned to her table.

Judge Anderson addressed the defense. "Mr. Parish, are you ready for your summation?"

"I am your honor."

"Proceed."

Jason patted Ellen's hand, stood and buttoned his suit coat. He smiled and approached the panel.

"As Ms. Cornwell so eloquently pointed out, my client, Ellen Morgan did, in fact, take her husband's life. That has never been disputed in these proceedings. She did shoot him to death while he lay in their marriage bed."

Two female jurors shuddered.

"That isn't a revelation. You've all seen the photographs and the shotgun that Ellen used to do the deed."

He put his hands on the railing in front of the jury and made eye contact with a woman in the second row and then an older man in the third row. "Did the defendant commit an act of deadly violence? Yes, she surely did." Jason stepped away from the jury and gestured toward Ellen. "Is there reasonable doubt about the commission of a capital crime? No, there is not."

Ellen covered her face with her hands.

Jason continued. "I remind the jury that the prosecution seeks the death penalty. All twelve of you must agree unanimously to return that verdict. The question here is not about what Mrs. Morgan did, but why she did it."

A murmur swept through the courtroom.

The attorney re-approached the panel. "Seven years of mental and physical abuse. Seven years of being used as a punching bag by the man

Ellen Morgan married and once loved. Seven years of having her dignity and self esteem battered again and again."

He made eye contact with a female juror who was fighting tears.

"You've all heard testimony from Ellen's family and saw the pictures of her injuries on the day she finally defended herself. Those were the result of a few of the countless beatings she suffered over the seven years of horror and fear."

Jason paused and pointed at the defendant. "To condemn that woman to death would be cruel and unusual punishment" He faced the jurors. "Ladies and gentlemen, I implore you to search your hearts and souls and return a verdict of not guilty."

Judge Anderson said, "Thank you counsel. It's four o'clock. The jury will be sequestered over night. Court is adjourned until nine o'clock tomorrow morning." She struck the gavel and a rush of voices filled the chamber.

Jason sat beside Ellen. She said, "I'm afraid."

He smiled and held her hand. "You're going to be all right."

* * * *

THE FOLLOWING MORNING
9:00 AM:

Again, the gallery was packed with Bert's associates, employees, friends and the press.

The bailiff said, "All rise."

Judge Anderson took the bench. "Be seated. This court is in session." She struck her gavel.

The jury filed in looking uneasy and tired.

"Has the jury reached a verdict?"

The foreperson cleared her throat. "No, your honor, we are hopelessly deadlocked."

A roar rose through the crowd.

"Order, or I'll clear the courtroom." She addressed the jury. "Would more time help reach a verdict?"

"We deliberated all night, your honor. We cannot reach a unanimous decision."

"Thank you for your time, you're excused." The judge addressed the attorneys. "I have no choice but to declare a mistrial." She continued. "Mrs. Morgan, would you please stand."

Ellen stood, shaking and crying.

"I cannot, nor will I ever condone what you have done. I encourage you to seek immediate, professional help and I pray that you can put your shattered life back together."

"Thank you, I believe I can do that now."

"This court is adjourned."

Author Note:

*R*eal stories like this do not always end with a hung jury. That was my way of handling the outcome. I didn't want my character to be found not guilty because it would not be realistic. To be given probation or a light sentence wouldn't work either. The deadlocked jury was the only justifiable conclusion.

Ellen did commit premeditated murder. Should we allow such retaliation to be tolerated? Think about it and I'm reasonably sure you'll agree, we should not.

There is a way out for battered women.

Bastard as he surely was, Bert was murdered. Regardless, that issue must be considered.

I produced an eight part radio series on battered woman. It was 1970, and images of most of those victims are not forgotten. The majority of my interviews were with married women who had found the courage to seek refuge in one of the shelters in San Diego California. They all told tales of horror and nearly every lady I talked to blamed herself and claimed to love the monsters who had beaten them.

Without a doubt, every single one of the sixty women in my study group had little or no self esteem.

Two months after the eighth show aired, I did a follow up report. Fifty of the women in my group had gone back to their men for more punishment.

One in particular came to mind when I started writing this story. She was an attractive twenty-nine-year-old woman married seven years to an older man. I get angry every time I recall her. She returned to her beast and he beat her to death on their eighth anniversary.

The scum that killed her got twenty-five to life. He was back on the street in fifteen.

Ted

A Forbidden Door

*I*n a moment everything changed. That fact has become the most frightening reality of my life.

* * * *

Tom Nelson and I were editing the final segment of a TV documentary on aging when the first ripple of my new reality hit the screen.

Creating illusion in video and on film is a matter of digital manipulation. It's part of my job and has been for years.

Carla Eagles, the hostess and expert of our documentary didn't need any slick electronics to do her thing. Carla's work wasn't illusion or magic–it was real.

Tom and I had a contract with EDTV to produce four one-hour segments for a show called, Questions. The series was our shot at the big-time. I kept my skeptical opinions to myself. We agreed to give the series our best–we needed the work.

My partner ran the last sequence of the video showing the face of an eighty-seven-year-old man. The old guy smiled, nodded and looked around with tears in his eyes. "Thank you," he said.

Mrs. Eagles gripped the old man's shoulder and faced the camera. "Mr. Collins has successfully completed a round trip to a long-past trauma. He faced it and erased the wounds."

The camera pulled back showing Carla and her patient cheek-to-cheek. Mrs. Eagles kissed the old gent on the forehead and wrapped the sequence. "Through the aid of hypnosis, step-by-step regression has eliminated a horrible memory from Mr. Collins' life, and he's become healthier as a result."

The camera cut to a close-up of the renewed patient. Tom froze the image and keyed the credits.

"Wait!" I grabbed his arm. "Back it up."

"For what?"

"I saw something. Take it back to the tight shot of Collins before Carla puts him under."

Tom reversed the tape … it was like Carla's therapy going back– regression.

"Go to slow motion. Right there. Freeze it."

The twenty-five inch monitor filled with Mr. Collins' aged face. I tapped the screen. "See it?"

My partner studied the screen. "What am I supposed to see?"

"The scar on his face."

"So what?"

"Run ahead, frame-by-frame, to where Eagles brings him out."

"What the hell are you looking for, Paul?"

"Do it. I know I saw it."

"The old man's coming around … what's to see?"

One frame at-a-time the pink scar on the left side of Mr. Collins' face faded. Several lines under his eyes fell away. Carla came into the shot. She kissed the man's cheek and pulled away. I tapped the screen again. "Freeze that frame."

Tom leaned closer to the monitor. "The scar's gone."

"Completely."

"It's not possible …." He touched the screen as if he could feel the old man's face. "He looks younger. Jesus, Paul–the guy looks younger."

"Yeah, younger, and with a non-surgical facelift as a bonus."

"This is weird. How could Eagles put one over on us?"

"I don't think she did." I marked the

frames on my editing sheet. "Cut in the credits. I'm calling Julia."

* * * *

Five minutes later I had the show's executive producer on the horn. "I need to expand the program, what's the big deal?"

"High six-figures, that's what. And how do I get additional air-time?"

"Negotiate, Julia, you're good at it."

"Last week you were wrapping. Now you want a fifth segment. What the hell are you up to?"

I pushed the old ego-button. "Get me the time and you'll be up for awards you haven't heard of yet."

"There won't be five shows, Paul–no way."

"Are you staring out the windows of your corner office like you do every time I ask for something?"

"Yes, wise guy. And dammit, I'm considering."

"You're a peach." I had her, the awards comment helped. "Here's the deal. I'll rework the last forty minutes of the stuff I've got and keep the project at four episodes." I held my breath. Julia's earrings clicked against the receiver.

"How much, Paul?"

"I'm looking at … say, two-hundred-thou."

"A hundred–tops."

"Deal … I love you."

She let out a long sigh. "what the hell have you got?"

Could I tell her I saw an old man grow younger? Not on my life, so I said, "The best thing since sliced bread."

Her earring clacked against the phone again. "Say it Paul."

"What … say what?"

"You always say it with every project."

"Oh–right … trust me."

"You're a royal pain in my ass."

"And you love it."

She hesitated, and then laughed in her special way. "I'll give you fifteen days–max."

"I'll deliver in ten." I swallowed a big mouthful of major responsibility right then. If I blew it–Tom and I were finished.

Julia slipped into her executive producer mode. "Just what are you into this time?"

"Youth, Julia … the honest-to-God fountain of youth."

"It better be good–I mean really good."

"Trust me … it's better than good."

"Fifteen days, one-hundred-thousand–no more."

"You're a gem. Love you–I'll be in touch."

* * * *

Tom stepped into my office. "What happened?"

"We got budget and two-weeks. I'm going to San Bernardino."

"You need me?"

"No, I want Carla's trust. I have to see her alone."

He slipped his bulk out and closed the door. I called Mrs. Eagles and arranged to see her the next afternoon.

* * * *

During the two-hour trip from San Diego to San Bernardino, I considered several ways to approach the subject of Carla regressing me. That was a twist. When we first started this production contract, I was less than polite about my thoughts on such nonsense. That was my first mistake. The second was thinking Mrs. Eagles didn't have both oars in the water. That opinion had changed real quick.

* * * *

Carla shook her head. "You're asking me to regress you for another show?"

"A few additional scenes, for clarity, that's it."

"Out of the question."

"Why the resistance?"

She looked away, studied the wall in her nicely furnished living room. After a moment she glared at me, eyes fixed, unblinking. Something she knew frightened her.

"My work is with people who need help." Carla leaned forward from her peach loveseat. "I'm not a carnival act, Mr. Clay–and you're not sick." She stood.

I got up. "Carla, I've changed my mind about you and what you do."

She stepped to the used-brick fireplace and leaned on the mantel. A wedding picture of her and her dead husband occupied a special place there. Carla looked at the gold-framed photograph and blinked rapidly. "Regression is a tool, a medicine."

"I think it's a door. It's a way back to a second chance."

"No–it's not!" Her voice cracked. Tears came.

I moved toward her. She turned away. "I suspected it from the first day of shooting, but I wouldn't let myself believe it."

"You're wrong!" She turned around. She had lied. "My work is professional hypnosis."

"Age regression. There's a difference, Carla. Your patients come back healthier."

"What would you know? You're a producer of TV shows–a non-believer."

"No. Not anymore. I saw the results of your

work. It's for real."

Mrs. Eagles faced her reflection in the mirror above the mantel. "I can't help you ... I'm sorry."

"What are you hiding?"

She crossed the room to the French windows on the opposite wall. Carla stared into the beautiful small flower garden beyond. "This meeting is over."

I had touched a nerve. "Not until you hear me out." I took the picture of Carla and her husband from the mantel and studied it. "How old are you?"

She tensed and turned away from the window. "What do you want from me?"

"Truth, nothing more. When was this picture taken?"

"Twenty years ago!" Carla turned away. "I was thirty." She looked back with tears in her eyes.

I put the picture on the coffee table and went to her. "You're the youngest looking fifty I've ever seen." I put my hands on her shoulders and whispered, "You haven't aged in twenty years. The closing shot in our last program shows your client getting younger. Not only did the old man wipe out his past trauma ... a physical scar of the incident disappeared with it." I hesitated. "Just tell me the truth."

She sighed. "Tissue ... please."

I handed her the small box of Kleenex from coffee table. I felt her tension drain away as she blotted her eyes and blew her nose. "I'm a friend, Carla … I care."

"Forgive me for being difficult, Paul." She wiped her eyes again. "I don't want to be seen as a joke."

"I would never show you that way, ever. You have my word." Carla was aching inside, I could feel a part of her pain.

She moved away from the window and went to the coffee table. "Regression is a door, Paul … just as you said." Carla picked up the picture and carried it back to the fireplace.

I measured my next question. "Have you've gone back a lot?"

"Yes … each time I get younger."

I walked around the coffee table. "How does that happen?" I sat in front of the fireplace.

Carla's gentle voice wavered. "I don't know." She stroked the picture with her slender fingers. "I take myself back to this moment." She studied the photo. "We talk. I don't try to change anything."

"What about the paradox, Carla?"

She laughed. "Meeting myself? There's no such problem." Her smile was radiant and her dark eyes filled with a soft glow. "I slip into myself at the moment of this picture and everything that was … is. The longer I stay, the younger I am when I come back."

I tried not to show it, but I shook inside. I was becoming a witness to something I could never explain. I had to see it and tried to understand. "When you're there, do you know what's going on?"

Carla touched the picture again and grinned. "Everything. I'm aware of it all. The future, the past and the present I left behind. I have complete control."

I nodded. "I want to believe you."

"Paul–I'm scared to death."

"Of what?" I was excited at the thought of what Carla might be able to do.

She walked away from the fireplace and sat on the arm of the love seat. "The last time I went back was a month ago." She turned her wedding ring around on her finger. "It was May twenty second. I stayed longer than usual. I lingered with the events following the picture. I remained for the wedding reception and our two-week honeymoon. We went on an Alaskan cruise. I lived it all again." Her voice wavered. "On the last night of the cruise, after Greg fell asleep, I came back." She shivered. "That frightened me."

"I'm trying to see it. What happened?"

"When I came back I was disoriented. I remembered getting into a hot bath. That's my most effective ways to regress." She hesitated. "I took that bath on May twenty second."

"And the whole session lasted for a few moments?"

"Not that time." She turned her wedding ring a few times and looked me right in the eyes. "When I returned, it was May eighth."

"Carla … that's incomprehensible."

"So is watching Mr. Collins' old scar disappear from his face." She smiled. "You saw it happen."

"I did, but rolling the present backward for over two weeks? That's science fiction."

"My present … only mine."

"There's no way I can pull something like this off in a TV show." I started pacing around the living room.

"Show?" She glared at me. "There won't be another show!" She stood. "I think you should leave now."

"I'm sorry … it's just hard to get my head around all of this."

"What you believe doesn't matter to me. You wanted truth and I'm giving it to you." She brushed silken black hair off her shoulders. "How or why it happens, I don't know, but it does."

At that moment, I wanted to hold her, tell her everything would be all right. I couldn't. Something beyond both of us was going to change my own reality. "Okay. Again, I apologize. Tell me how it was when you came back, I want to understand."

"As I told you, The regression in May was the longest I allowed myself to experience." She looked at me for a moment.

"Yes, go on. I'm with you."

"You're dying to take notes."

"May I?"

"Be sure you get it right. There won't be another chance."

"Excuse me?"

"I won't be available after today."

"I'm not following."

"You will."

She walked to the French Windows and stared out at her flower garden. The afternoon light made the woman a tall attractive silhouette. I wanted a shot of that, but I hadn't brought a camera.

Carla looked toward me for a brief moment. "When I returned from the honeymoon, as I told you, I reentered the present, my present, more than two-weeks earlier than when I had left." She shuddered. "The longest I'd been gone before was a little more than a day." She went back to the love seat and sat down. "Nothing was any different when I came back." She looked at me through a serious expression. "The May event changed all that."

I jotted a note. "What was different about it?"

"There's always a few moments of blurred vision and a sense of floating. I'm usually sitting in the tub and the water's cooled down." She took a breath. "Not that time. I was sitting at the kitchen table staring at an arrangement of fresh flowers."

"That's significant?"

Carla got up and stood by the fireplace. "I had put those flowers in the trash a week before my regression." She touched the wedding picture. "The clock radio displayed 3:30 PM:May/8."

Everything Carla had told me could have been an elaborate fabrication. However, I had a gut feeling it wasn't. "What happened after May eighth?"

She looked off into an opposite corner of the room. "I floated through each day in a state of apprehension. Everything was vague, yet familiar at the same time. It was like … a parallel existence. Then I came to May twenty-second--the hot bath." Carla stiffened. "I shot right back to Greg and the wedding reception. It all started again." Her eyes widened, she swallowed hard and drew a deep breath. "I forced myself back. Back to my present. She twisted her wedding ring again. "I haven't regressed since–I'm afraid."

"You're scaring the hell out of me." I shook it away for the moment, but a touch of doubt crossed my mind.

"I'm subtracting the present from my life. I'm returning to the past, going backward a little at-a-time. When I return it's earlier in my life." She wrung her hands and stared at the floor.

"You okay?" I leaned forward and just let the question come out. "With all the expertise you have, isn't it possible that all of this is going on in your mind like a recurring dream?"

"That's logical. I would expect you to think that."

"I didn't mean to doubt you."

"It's all right, I understand." She hesitated. "You're absolutely correct. My regression therapy works within a patient's repressed memory."

"I have no intention to dismiss or demean what you do. Give me the benefit of the doubt here, it's not easy to accept."

Carla looked at me and smiled. Tears rimmed her eyes. "Paul ... the time has come when I can relive my life with Greg forever."

I must've stared at her for several moments before responding. "You said, has come."

"I don't need the hot bath to trigger my regressions anymore. I've developed the process to work through my own resolve."

"Okay. So, you think about an event and off you go."

Her eyes brightened and she answered, "Not quite that simple, but basically, you're right."

"What do you do, close your eyes and concentrate?"

Her face lit up. "I can do that. In fact, I've been doing so over the past two months."

"You said you hadn't gone back since the May event."

"I haven't. I've learned to regress slowly without going all the way." She closed her eyes and touched the wedding picture. 'I'm regressing right now. This time, I won't be coming back."

"What are you saying?" I stood and almost toppled the chair. "You're going now?"

"Yes, today. I've considered it since doing your show. Now, after sharing with you, I believe it's time."

"I don't need a demonstration, Carla, I believe you—I really do." She was so full of life and spirit. I wanted to shake her and pull the woman out of her regression. I realized that would be a mistake. "You have a life here."

"What I have here are memories from a life I lost. My abilities allow me to have another chance."

I had major problems with everything she was telling me. Questions hung in the air like smoke at a backroom poker game. "What happens to the lovely Carla Eagles standing in this room right now?"

"You're charming." She came up to me and touched my face. "I really don't know. I suppose I'll cease to be." She grinned. "At least here, in this time."

I held her hand for a few seconds. "You're cold."

She nodded. "That's a good sign. My regression is working."

My thoughts started racing. I became concerned and upset with her. "Okay, Carla—dammit! What if you don't go anywhere and just shutdown and die? Is that what this is really all about?"

"I'm touched." She held my hand in both of hers and they had become colder. "I assure you, I have no intention of dying." She put my hand against her cool cheek. "I'm going to live a long new life with Greg."

At that moment I wanted to hug her and beg her to stop the regression. Instead, I became angry. "All right, Mrs. Eagles—you go off into the cosmos. Forget about Mr. Collins and the battered women and those abused children you helped during our documentary. Let them suffer their traumas again and again!"

Carla held me.

"You're more of a caring person than I thought." She kissed me on the cheek. "The people I've worked with, including the ones on the TV shows, will not be changed when I'm gone. The regression, in each patient, was theirs, not mine."

I thought about how stupid it would sound and then asked anyway. "What about your body? Will I have to call 911 and try to explain how I happen to be in the house with a dead woman?"

Her laugh sounded hollow.

"Actually, I don't know, but I doubt that any trace of me will remain."

That didn't set well and I started getting a bit apprehensive. "Maybe I should disappear and let you drift off to join Greg in private."

"I want you to stay with me and witness my passing."

"That sounds an awful lot like death."

"It won't be. Please stay."

There wasn't a shred of evidence that I'd see anything. The thought of what might happen shook me to the bone.

"I may try to stop you." Something changed in her expression. "I kind of like having you around."

"You won't be able to stop my regression. It's already gone beyond return."

Her physical presence changed. I thought it was the light. She had less color in her face.

"Are you okay?"

She grinned. "I'm getting weaker."

I stepped toward her. "What haven't you told me?"

She took my hand. "Let's go to the kitchen, I'll make some coffee."

Her hand had become as cold as ice. I helped her step slowly out of the living room.

"Okay, coffee. I want the rest of the story with it,"

* * * *

Mrs. Eagle's kitchen came right out of *House Beautiful.*

"Your husband passed twenty-years ago?"

"Greg died one month after our second anniversary." Carla poured bottled water into her Bunn coffee maker. "His death led me to my regression therapy, which I added to my psychology practice."

Though she was dressed in jeans, sneakers and, obviously, one of her late-husband's shirts, which she had tied in a knot at the waist, Carla's elegance was apparent. I weighed my comment, then voiced it. "Eighteen years is a long time to be alone."

"Alone?" She pushed back a lock of curly, black hair. "You heard my story, I'm not alone."

Her smiling glance caught my red face. "Right ... you're not." I wanted to say something else. Whatever it was, I can't remember. This woman had drawn my entire focus. I was overwhelmed by the aura of her sexuality. Carla had the essence of some glowing power that pulsated just under the surface. At that moment I wanted to hold her--take some of her energy into myself, and just maybe slip back through time. I shivered. Like an idiot, I just stared.

Carla smiled. She knew what I was thinking. She pulled two mugs down from the cupboard. "You can't, Paul, not with me, but I'm pleased at the thought."

"I'm sorry. Christ, I feel like an moron."

"I'm flattered. Would you like cream and sugar?"

Embarrassed, I nodded. "Please. You seem better than you were when we left the living room."

She put the mugs on the highly-polished picnic table that served as a breakfast nook. "I've slowed down the regression so we could have more time. You asked for the whole story and I want you to hear it. I make love with Greg every time I go back." Carla slipped into the nook across from me and sipped her coffee. "It's as satisfying as it ever was."

I stirred two teaspoons of sugar and a dash of cream into my coffee. "I'm fascinated by all of it, Carla–way beyond the TV show. I mean that … really."

"Regression is mental not physical. You caught on to it earlier. Whatever I share with Greg, when I go back, is in my mind. At least that's what it's been so far."

"Somehow … I think there's more to it."

"You're always probing. That's really you, isn't it?"

"Yes, and I'm good at it." I took a sip of coffee before I went on. I didn't want to push her. "Why are you afraid? You've regressed many times."

"Afraid? Yes, I am."

"You've said that several times, now I see

it in your eyes … what is it?"

She left the table to get us fresh coffee. "There *is* a paradox, Paul."

I knew there had to be a glitch somewhere and I wanted to hear it. "I suspected as much."

She returned to the table, sat down and poured fresh brew. "It scares me to death." She shook back her hair and ticked her nails on her cup. "When I regress briefly … a few hours, even a whole day, I can't see it." She stared off into the bright kitchen.

"Can't see what?"

She whispered, "The ghost, the real paradox." Carla took a short breath and shuddered. "It was always there, I felt it, but couldn't quite detect it." She held her cup in both hands again. "I know how this must sound to you."

"I'm not here to judge."

She looked at me for a moment.

"I didn't want to see, I suppose, but I knew something was happening. It got stronger. I saw the ghost. I saw it, Paul!"

"Okay, I'm listening." Her conviction was absolute. Whatever doubts I had were rapidly falling away.

She slid out of the booth again and put the pot back under the coffee maker and leaned against the counter. "Let's not call it a paradox, or a ghost … an image. That's good enough."

"It's your vision. Call it whatever you want."

"No–not a vision either." She studied me for a moment, and then turned back to the sunlight streaming in through the kitchen window. "I've lived with the damn thing for the last three weeks." Her voice was distant, haunted. Through the louvers and the oak shutters Carla was segmented in light and shadow.

"Image is fine." I made a mental note to duplicate the same lighting effect in the studio. It would be a nice touch, but I knew it wouldn't involve Carla."

"As I told you, when I came back from my last experience, I had returned two-weeks before the regression." She tilted her head back, closed her eyes. "I was already here."

"Again, please, I was writing notes."

"There were two of me …."

"You saw yourself?"

"It was like the soft flutter of lace curtains at an open window." She stared into the sunlight. "I was moving in a kind of dream-state. I tingled all over."

"Did you hear anything?"

"There was a presence in front of me … faint impressions–no sounds."

Her voice drifted away–so did her image. "Carla–you're fading out!"

"What?" She turned toward me regarding

my presence as if I'd just appeared in her kitchen. "Paul?"

Something held me back from approaching her. I think I was afraid she'd shatter or disappear. "We're talking about the image, Carla … c'mon, sit down."

"More coffee?" She went for the pot as if she'd just left the table.

"Please sit down." I took the pot from her as she slid back into the booth. I filled her mug, pushed it toward her. "You were shimmering away there for a minute."

"I was going back … I could see her–me."

"Drink some coffee. Keep your eyes open and tell me what just happened."

She shivered.

"You feel chilled?"

"Yes."

"I think you do because of what's in your head."

"I was feeling that first day … and just now …."

She started drifting again. "Look, Carla, maybe this isn't such a great idea. You're having problems here because I've kind of forced you into it."

"No, it's time, Paul … I'm going back. Please stay with me."

"I don't know what to do." I never felt so helpless in my life.

"Get me to the bedroom." She pressed her fingers to both temples. Her face turned ashen-gray.

"You're fading—stop the regression."

"I can't. The bedroom, I need to lie down."

"Are you in pain?"

"My head. The bedroom. Down the hall to the right—don't leave me, Paul."

"Not a chance." I pulled her out of the booth and carried her to the bedroom. She felt as light as a ten-year-old. I was frightened to the core.

* * * *

"My head is splitting … I have to lie down."

"Here, I'm putting you on the bed. Stay with me."

"My head–pounding. A towel with ice in it, please."

Carla's face had gone white. I could feel her pain. "I'll get the towel–hold on."

"I'm going, Paul … this is the worst. It'll be over soon."

"I'll be back in a minute don't go, Carla–wait!"

"Close the blinds … please … the light."

"Okay." I fumbled with the cords and drew the blinds and drapes.

"Thank you … it's better." She covered her eyes and pressed her thumbs against her temples.

I felt a sense of guilt and rushed toward the kitchen. *I caused this.* I thought. *All for the damn TV show.* I scooped ice cubes from the fridge into a dish towel and ran back to the bedroom. I stopped short.

Everything in the room had turned gray. She was sitting up, smiling.

"Are you all right?"

"I'm ready now … there's no more pain."

I dropped the towel full of ice. It vanished instantly. "Carla, take my hand."

"No, I can't … I'm going to be with Greg."

"Grab hold of me. You have a life here!"

"Don't touch me, Paul. You'll be lost if you do. I wanted you to see this happen it's real. My life is with Greg and our future together." Her raven hair fell over her shoulders. She looked no more than twenty-five, then twenty and fading.

I swear I heard distant music and voices. At that point, I couldn't be sure of anything except what I actually witnessed. Carla had become transparent. She spoke in my head.

Thank you for helping me.

"She was gone. The room was empty–no furniture, no drapes–nothing."

I stumbled back through the hallway into the empty, kitchen. "Carla!" My voice bounced off the walls. No shiny picnic table or coffee maker.

The fridge doors were open and there was no light on inside.

Beams of Light from the setting sun streamed into the living room through naked windows. I shouted, "Carla!"

Nothing.

I caught the glint of a refection from the fireplace. Carla's wedding picture was still there. I rushed to the mantel. When I reached for the photograph it faded away. "Carla!"

Her voice whispered across the empty room like a soft breeze on an August afternoon. "I'm home now, Paul. I'm with Greg for always."

"Carla!" There was nothing more.

I stood in the middle of an empty room. Mrs. Eagles and everything she owned had vanished. Carla was nonexistent. She didn't live in my time any longer. She had regressed thirty-years into her past, and had not yet lived in this house.

* * * *

I let myself out through the front door. My car was still parked in the driveway. That much was for real. I looked back at the vacant house and stared at the sign that wasn't there before. It was stuck on a metal post in the front yard:

FOR SALE
LENNOX REALTY
CALL FOR APPOINTMENT
858-555-6354

* * * *

On the drive back to San Diego, I left a message on Julia's answering machine:

"I'm glad you're out. This won't make much sense anyway. Forget the extra budget. The show goes as is. I was dead wrong. There isn't any fountain of youth. Love you bunches. Bye."

I clicked off my cell. "God bless you, Carla … give my best to Greg."

The Last Job

*C*huck Martin took a sip from his Jim Beam. "When this is over, I'm out for good, gone, history."

Tim Corey grinned and lit another cigarette. "If it goes down clean you can do what you want."

"If it doesn't we'll both be history."

"You have your people in place, I have mine. Everybody's an adult, the risks are understood."

"A few details are shaky."

A cold October wind shook the windows of the warehouse office. "Not on my end." Tim crushed out his smoke.

"The taking of the eighteen-wheeler is the trouble spot."

Tim poured more JB for both of them. "We've been over it a dozen times."

"Yeah. I'd like to run through it again."

"You're serious?"

"Bet your ass."

Tim sat back and lit another smoke. "Nailing the semi bothers you?"

"It does."

"One hour and twenty minutes after the truck leaves the Dallas distribution center the driver gets to our bogus roadblock. One of my phony State Troopers approaches the cab and asks for the trip sheet and ID. Tim took a sip of JB. "Mike knocks on the passenger door and says he has to look inside."

"There's the problem."

"What?"

"Good old boy, Mike. You brought him in after the setup was in place."

"He's a driver, he can handle the rig."

"I don't give a shit about his driving skills." Chuck threw back his drink. "He's an ex-con! He has a wrap-sheet as long as your arm–all of it for assault and robbery."

"Mike's not a choir boy."

"My men aren't either, but they've never been busted, never done time. That's why my jobs are always clean."

"I can't pull him off now. If I do, he'll cause trouble we don't want."

Chuck leaned forward. "If that truck driver is roughed up or worse, good old Mike will be one sorry sonofabitch–that's a promise."

"Easy." Tim poured more booze. "The driver will be gassed and Mike takes the truck and five-hundred-thousand worth of stamped cigarettes right into this warehouse." He chuckled. "What the hell do you care anyway? Your crew transfers the goods to my tractor-trailer." Tim nodded toward the Kenworth parked in the warehouse. "My people are standup guys. They'll get the job done right."

"That's what I thought before I knew you had a convict in a key role." He leaned back. "Face it, most of your hired help couldn't make it through a thirty second lineup on a burglary beef. They're cheap hoods you bail out. They don't concern me as much as dirt bag Mike. This nut beat-up on a guard at Huntsville and you pulled strings to get him out."

"You sure have a lot of inside information I don't remember sharing with anyone recently."

"I find out what I have to going in with somebody on any job. I'm not comfortable with your driver selection. If the legit driver puts up a fight he could be a dead man."

"Forget it, Chuck. The empty semi and its sleeping driver will bc found in a rest stop on the Interstate. He won't remember a thing."

"That had better be the case. I'll be here

Monday night to supervise the transfer of cargo. I need to see an unharmed, living driver when Mike pulls in."

Monday 10:30 PM:

Tim and Mike were enjoying a drink in the warehouse office when Chuck came in. "Gentlemen." He flashed his ATF badge. "You're under arrest for hijacking, kidnapping a federal officer and possession of stolen goods." To the original truck driver he said. "John, cuff 'em and read them their rights." To Tim he said, "I guess this is your last job. Mine just got started."

A Day of Summer's End

"We're comin' up on Quarry Creek!" Charlie Walker yelled into the clamor of noise and rushing wind.

The boxcar clanked and rocked. The train eased into a long, slow curve.

Buddy Miller leaned against the opposite side of the open doorway. "Let's jump off here an' go swimming."

Charlie gulped down the rest of his stale beer. "No way. We're goin' on to Jefferson Station like we said."

It was the last Saturday of summer vacation. The boys would remember that day for the rest of their lives.

Charlie tossed out his empty bottle and watched it smash against a cluster of passing rocks.

Buddy took a swallow of warm brew and made a face. "Hey, that was cool!" He threw his bottle, but no smash. It bounced off a wooden pole.

The older boy shook his head. "Aim for the rocks, dummy."

"I hit the pole didn't I?"

"Yeah, but the bottle didn't bust."

"What are you getting mad at?"

Charlie hunkered down against a wall of cardboard containers. "I was thinking about school and not being together this year ... you know."

"Yeah ... it ain't gonna be like it was anymore." Buddy heaved another bottle out the door and scored a bust.

Come Monday, Buddy would start ninth grade. Charlie was one year ahead and he was going to another school. They were being separated for the first time since they knew each other.

Buddy looked at his best friend. "You'll get in with new kids and a bunch of other stuff."

"Not so. Besides, we can be together after school, like always."

"It won't be like that, Charlie. Those guys over at Morison are older like you. They don't want no little kid hanging around and you know it."

"I promise. It's you an' me. The Morison

guys are rich brats. They wouldn't have the guts to do shit like we do." He laughed and swigged a gulp of beer. "Cheer up, Buddy—we're on an adventure."

It had been the older boy's notion to hop the train and ride into Jefferson for the day. The whole idea became even better when the car they jumped on turned out to be loaded with half and quarter-full bottles of beer. They were stacked, in heavy cartons, on each end of the boxcar. There was plenty of space for the boys in the middle.

This was sure to be the most exciting Saturday of the whole summer.

* * * *

Just over an hour later the train rocked, shook and slowed again.

Charlie choked on a swallow of stale beer. "This is Jefferson."

Buddy took a sip from his bottle and threw it out the door. "Yuck, that's enough of that stuff." He wiped his sleeve across his mouth. "I gotta eat or I'm gonna throw up."

Charlie stood and looked out toward the head-end of the long train. "Holy shit!" He ducked back in. "Quick, get up against the boxes and be quiet."

The boys pressed themselves into the shadows as far as they could.

"Can't we get off?" Buddy spoke in a whisper.

"They're changing crews here–shut up an' sit tight."

The train screeched, clanged, banged and jerked, then stopped.

Swirls of dust whispered through the rays of hot sun that beamed through the open door.

Everything went still.

Rapid heartbeats rose in two small chests.

"Charlie Walker–we're gonna get caught!" Buddy's voice was scratchy, tight and dry.

"Be quiet and listen." He pulled his legs up tighter to make himself smaller.

Buddy held his breath.

"There's somebody coming toward this car." Charlie's words came out on a cracked whisper.

Buddy said, "God–we're busted!"

Heavy footsteps crunched the ballast along the tracks, and then stopped.

Shuffling sounds.

Mumbling.

A man's voice.

Slam.

A huge, dark blue valise landed on the wood floor and slid to the center of the boxcar.

Two young heads jerked back and four startled eyes stared at the object in awe.

Buddy swallowed and it made a click in his throat.

Charlie froze and shivered.

The case was made of heavy leather and carpet. It strained at the seams to hold its contents. An elaborate needlework formed a profiled face of a quarter moon. It was centered in a circle of stars. The eyes of the satellite were closed and the mouth turned downward in a sullen expression. Each of the four corners of the tapestry displayed a ringed planet resembling Saturn.

The boys held their collective breaths.

A figure of a large man appeared in the doorway. His back was to the sun and he looked like a dark shadow with unusually bright eyes.

The shadow blinked.

The boys shook.

With one quick pull the dark form stepped up into the boxcar. He leaned over and grabbed his case. He set it back against the stacked cartons and turned slowly into the sunlight and faced the two boys.

They drew short breaths.

The lined and weathered face of the tall stranger wrinkled up into a warm, friendly smile. He chuckled softly and adjusted his dusty, well-worn top-hat. A rumpled dark gray suit hung loosely about his large frame. It made him appear fat, which he was not. He shaded his glowing eyes with his thick, hard hand and brought it down from the brim of his hat.

"Couple more passengers, I detect, in the corner shadows there."

Two rapid hearts skipped a beat at the same time.

"Good." The strange visitor continued. "I like company on a long train ride." He reached for the carpet bag and four eyes shifted with his movement. "Allow me to introduce myself." The strange man nodded. "I am William Jonathan Mulligan at your service." He tipped his hat and winked.

A prickly cold centipede bristle shot up Buddy's back. The shiver opened his mouth in a gape.

Charlie clenched his fists. The lump in his throat made his eyes water. "I can't breathe." The boy's words were a slight whisper.

The quarter moon on the big man's case became full. Its eyes opened wide and the frown turned upside down.

When the moon-face winked Buddy started for the door. Charlie made a dash in the same direction.

William Jonathan Mulligan reached out and blocked the escape. "I wouldn't do that just yet boys."

They stopped, eyes bulged, hearts in their throats. Their heads shook with each heartbeat.

"Railroad men are marching toward this car on both sides." Mr. Mulligan grinned. His bright eyes blinked again. "We have two choices. Hide or get nailed."

The youngsters looked at each other through wide-eyed milk-white faces. They shifted their glances to the stranger, who talked like a friend.

Mr. Mulligan lifted his mystery bag to the top of the stacked cartons and gave it a hefty shove. He smiled, "Hide or make a break for it."

Quick footsteps on the cinders and men's voices came closer to the open doors.

The boys spun around and made an attempt to climb the stacked containers.

In an instant, two strong hands raised them over the first row of boxes and into the shadows. Charlie and Buddy lay flat and still and each held his breath.

Charlie peeked over the cartons–Mr. Mulligan was gone.

One rough-looking railroad man leaned into one side of the boxcar. "This one's clear."

Another man peered into the opposite door. "Looks clear to me–lock her up."

Buddy sucked air and made a noise.

Charlie clamped his hand over his friend's mouth. "Quiet."

Whatever sound Buddy might have made could not have been heard.

A thunderous, scraping rumble vibrated the air in the boxcar.

Bright rays of warm sun were replaced with a cold darkness.

The huge doors *slammed* shut!

* * * *

"Charlie." Buddy's voice shot into black space. "We're trapped!"

"No we ain't. I'll get the door open."

"How?"

"I said I'd do it. Stop whining." Charlie slid his legs over the edge of the stacked cartons.

Rivulets of cold sweat crept down the younger boy's back. The weight of darkness pressed on him like a foul shroud. He shivered and wiped at his tears.

Charlie dropped to the floor with a thud and made his way to the side wall of the boxcar. He reached out with groping fingers in wide-eyed blindness and shuffled forward.

"You okay?" Buddy hadn't moved an inch. Dark hung heavy–fear too thick.

"Yeah," answered Charlie. "You?"

Buddy shifted his eyes back and forth, up and down. There wasn't any difference between eyes open or eyes shut. "I'm okay …."

A loose bottle spun at the bump of Charlie's sneaker. It rolled against the steel door with a loud clank. He worked his way to an inside handle. "I found a latch." The boy grabbed the handle with both hands and gave it a hefty yank.

Nothing.

Buddy pulled himself to the edge of the containers. "You gotta get us out, Charlie."

Rattling and shaking echoed through the lightless freight car.

"It won't budge—dammit!"

The tiny hairs on the back of Buddy's neck stood straight up. He blinked in the dark and swallowed against the pressure in his throat. He remembered cold sweats and spider dreams on thunderstorm August nights. *My flashlight,* he said in his mind. *Such a magic it is,* the young boy thought. It chased the night away. Under the covers Buddy could see and not be seen. "I wish I had my light." Buddy spoke out loud without meaning to.

"What?" Charlie tugged and shook the lever once more.

"I wish we never got on this rotten train." Buddy's words sounded strained and choked. *Don't cry,* he thought. He didn't.

"Stop being a baby; I'll get us out." Charlie pounded and kicked the door as though it would do some good.

"All that hammering and banging is going to scrape your knuckles and give the rest of us a headache."

The boys stared at Mr. Mulligan's bright eyes high in the blackness. He was at the opposite end of the boxcar.

"It is light we need and light we shall have." The stranger blinked and the glow in his eyes disappeared.

The boys listened to Mr. Mulligan's rustling and shuffling.

Charlie squatted and leaned against the unyielding door.

A blue-white glow began to chase away the pitch dark.

What had been the needle-work moon on the old man's carpetbag changed into a bright sun. The stars and planets in the field behind it faded.

Cold darkness was gone.

Charlie jumped to his feet and grabbed the lever. "Open!"

The train lurched and picked up speed. The door didn't move.

"We're stuck now, Charlie an' it's your fault." Buddy mumbled his protest into the wall of boxes. He didn't want his friend or the stranger to see the tears in his eyes.

"No we ain't. I'll get us out at the next stop." Charlie kicked the steel door again.

Mr. Mulligan climbed down from the wall of boxes. "Won't be a stop for quite some time."

"How do you know?" The older boy wasn't

quite sure of a strange man who could make moon and sun come and go on a carpetbag.

"This train is headed for the middle of America, my boy. That's where green hills follow country roads through quiet towns. It's a place where sweaty, devilish young boys seek adventures. They're just like you. They'll do anything–anything at all. They wish to make this day of summer's end last longer than the whole summer itself." The big man laughed.

Charlie watched the strange man's shadow move on the wall of the swaying boxcar.

Buddy saw it at the same time. They both drew short breaths.

The form was not the outline of a man in a bulky suit and wrinkled top-hat. It was the image of a long robe and a wizard's cone-shaped headwear. The glowing eyes of the stranger were projected into the black shadow–they blinked.

"Don't let that old thing scare you." Mr. Mulligan chuckled. He took a carton down from the stack behind him and sat on it. He moved out of the light and the apparition vanished.

The boys looked back at the huge man.

"That's just the harmless image of an old wish of mine. Sometimes, he's a good friend."

Charlie glanced back at the wall. "A wish?"

"Just a dream." Mr. Mulligan leaned back against the containers and pulled his top-hat forward. "I wanted to be something I was not. I

I wanted it free without effort,"

Charlie shook his head and smirked. "What's that got to do with a dumb shadow?"

"Look at the wall again and you'll see." The old man crossed his strong arms and grinned.

The silhouette of Charlie showed a full grown man with an empty space in the center of its chest.

"That ain't my shadow."

"It is, son … sure as you are, it is." Mr. Mulligan turned to catch Buddy's eye and winked.

"There's a hole in Charlie's shadow." He pointed at his. "Mine doesn't have one."

"That's because you don't wish to be anything but what you are." Mr. Mulligan's bright eyes twinkled. "You're just a young boy going into the ninth grade and that's all you want to be right now."

"What about mine?" Charlie reached up and touched his shadow. It remained tall and moved with him. "Why is it so big?"

"It is your wish." Mr. Mulligan touched the valise and the sun grew brighter. "You want to be a man and you're not."

"Why is there a hole?" He put up his hand to shade the empty space. "It won't go away."

"There's no heart in a man who has not first lived as a boy." The old man stood and his wizard shadow rose with him and appeared between those of the Boy's. "A man cannot be a man without first being a boy." He put his thick, strong hands on the youngster's shoulders. The image on the wall did the same to the smaller shadows beside it. "When the boy has been all the boy he can be," continued Mr. Mulligan. "When he has done all the boy things he can do, then the boy becomes a man." He squeezed two small shoulders. "Then and only then will the boy be a grown man with a full heart."

Buddy leaned forward and touched the tips of his shadow's fingers. "What happens to the boy?"

"Whatever the boy was, and all the fine things he did, live on in the center of his man-heart."

They swayed with the rhythm of the rocking train and stared at their tell-tale shadows.

Mr. Mulligan gripped each of the boy's small shoulders tighter. The bright eyes of the wizard-shadow blinked.

Buddy studied his friend's heartless image. "Will Charlie's shadow ever have a heart?"

"If he stops trying to be a man and lives as a boy, yes. It sure will."

The older lad looked up into Mr. Mulligan's shining eyes. "Why is your shadow different from thc way you look?"

"Because of my youthful impatience." He laughed. "As a boy, I wanted to be a magician so I played at magic. It wasn't enough to do card

card tricks."

Mr. Mulligan took his hand off Charlie's shoulder and produced an ace of spades.

The boy's eyes widened. The weathered hand turned once and the card was gone. "Pulling rabbits out of hats soon became boring." He removed his bent top-hat and the youngsters stepped back. Mr. Mulligan winked, gave a wide grin and reached into the hat. His knuckles struck the inside of the topper with a thump. A small cloud of ancient dust shook loose. "I'll have to get that cleaned one of these days."

In one swift move, the big man raised a red-eyed white rabbit high above his head. "Quick, look at my shadow!"

The opposite arm of the wizard-shadow was held high.

Charlie yelled. "The rabbit's gone!"

Mr. Mulligan's hand was empty.

"The rabbit never was, my friends ... it was just an illusion." He turned his hand from side-to-side, and then brought it down slowly.

"But I saw the card and the rabbit." Buddy looked right, then left and up into the dark space above the stacked boxes.

"You saw the card and the rabbit in your mind. That's how magic works." He knocked more dust from his hat. "Being a magician wasn't good enough for me. I wished to be a wizard." He smiled and put the wrinkled hat back on his head.

"Why a wizard?" Charlie had a sharp tone in his voice. He yanked down a cardboard carton and sat on it.

Buddy squatted against a stack of containers.

"A wizard is something special," continued the old man. "A wizard can wave his arms and frogs become dragons. A seasoned wizard can fill a black sky with stars. He can turn winter into summer. Now that is a wizard." Mr. Mulligan waved his arms as he spoke. His gestures were amplified by his strange shadow. "Yes, I wanted to be a wizard. I didn't want to earn it–I just wished and wanted."

Buddy brushed a lock of sweaty, red hair from his brow. "Can you ever be a wizard?"

"I can if I help enough people by answering needs instead of wants." He blinked and his bright eyes twinkled. "You have a need that's why I'm here."

"You can help us?" Buddy's eyes brightened.

"Have you both forgotten? You're trapped in this boxcar and we're long past where you wanted to get off."

"C'mon, mister, you're a railroad bum with a bag of phony tricks and tall stories." He jumped to his feet and pulled a half-full bottle of beer out of an open case.

The clacking and rocking of the speeding

train became more apparent in the absence of conversation.

Goose bumps crawled up Buddy's arms when he heard the hollow ring of a crossing- bell rush by. "We're way past Jefferson Station by now. What can you do, Mr. Mulligan?"

"If you believe in me, I can help." He snapped his thick fingers and waved his arms. His wizard-shadow did the same. "You see–that's the catch." He shook his head and adjusted his dusty hat. "You have to believe." The big man leaned closer to Buddy. "Deep down inside, you must be convinced that, I–William Jonathan Mulligan, granter of dreams and man of magic, can fill your need."

Charlie snickered and spit beer on the floor. "You're a funny old man, but you ain't no wizard."

Buddy's eyes widened. He blinked once and whispered, "I believe …."

The magic man raised his arms again and lifted his head high. "I'll stop this train where you wanted it to be and I'll open the doors of this car!"

Charlie laughed and gulped a swallow of warm beer. "I'll believe it when I see it, pops."

Buddy said, "Shut up, Charlie." The small boy looked up at the tall stranger. "I believe you can do it, Mr. Mulligan ... please—do it!"

The strange man of magic shook his head again. "Belief wouldn't be necessary if I were a wizard–only a need." He winked at Buddy and walked to the center of the rocking boxcar.

Mr. Mulligan cupped his rugged chin. "A wizard," he said, over the clatter-clanking of the rumbling train, "would lift his arms into the air." He raised his arms and continued. "A wizard would call upon the power of the stars. He would pull down the energy of the sun and command these doors to open to its light."

The old man closed his eyes tight and clenched his fists. His arms stiffened. His face vibrated with strain.

Nothing happened.

Charlie laughed.

Buddy took a quick breath, closed his eyes and whispered, "Please, I believe. Open the door …."

Nothing.

Charlie laughed again. "You two would make great circus clowns."

The train rattled on.

Mr. Mulligan clenched is fists tighter. His face began to sweat.

The doors held.

Buddy yelled above the clamor. "Open, you lousy, rotten door–now!" He had raised his arms and clenched his fists, just like Mr. Mulligan.

Clank–scrape–rattle. One door shook.

Charlie coughed on a guzzle of beer. His laughing ceased.

A drop of sweat ran down the big man's Roman nose and fell to the wooden floor.

Buddy stared wide-eyed and sucked air through his teeth.

SLAM.

The sound echoed through the swaying car.

The latch let loose.

The heavy, steel door shot open and rammed against its stops.

Daylight, dust and hot wind filled the boxcar with the fury of a summer storm.

Charlie shaded his eyes and fell back hard against the wall of cartons. "Holy, shit!" He dropped the bottle. "The door's open!" His words were blown away in the raging wind.

"You did it, Mr. Mulligan–you did it!" The excited sounds of Buddy's words were nearly covered by the noise.

"We did it, young man. We did it, because you believed." He stood hatless in the blast of train-made wind. His glowing eyes blinked. "Lord of the sky—man in the moon. Light of forgotten stars—I've earned my dream!" A trickle of sweat ran into the corner of the old man's widening smile. He lowered his arms and the baggy sleeves of his gray coat slipped over his wrists. He shook back his strewn white hair and grinned into the blazing sunlight. "We've done a wizard's task." He nodded. "We have at that." The racing air chased his words through the boxcar.

Charlie brushed himself off and stepped away from the boxes. "Open the other one." He raised his voice over the decreasing wind.

"One's enough, son … never ask for more than you need." He picked up his hat and slapped it twice against his leg. A new cloud of dust scattered into the wind.

"Can you stop the train?" Buddy brushed his red locks away from his face. "Can you?"

"I might be able to get us back to where all this started, but first things first."

Mr. Mulligan waved his hand toward the bright sun on his carpetbag. It changed back to a full moon and smiled down on them. "No need for two suns, is there?" He winked. "Have you boys got a quarter each?" He held out his bent top-hat.

"I do." Buddy jingled the change in his pocket. "I was saving it for an ice cream, but you can have it." He held out the coin.

"Drop it in the hat, lad." Mr. Mulligan nodded as the quarter landed inside.

Charlie reached into both pants pockets. "Yeah, I got one." He dropped the second coin into the old hat. "What'd you want the money for?"

"A token, my friends. A token of my gratitude to the both of you."

The boys looked at each other through expressions of confusion, then back to Mr. Mulligan.

He jingled the coins in the hat three times.

"Secrets of the moon, I beg your strength." He shook the quarters again. "Bind these two for all of childhood's length. Set them free so they may run. Let them run until they are men. Until then, they'll remain as one." He opened his eyes and smiled.

Buddy poked Charlie and the boys stepped back.

The big man held out his scrubby hat. A blue mist rose from the inside, and vanished in the wind.

"Take them, they're yours to keep."

The boys hesitated."

"Go ahead. They're my gifts to you." He tapped the rim of the hat, the coins jingled. "Be sure to examine them carefully."

First Buddy, then Charlie took a coin from the hat. Each quarter felt warm and new. On the face side, of what had been ordinary quarters, appeared a bright-eyed quarter moon with a radiant smile. It gleamed in a field of stars.

Charlie turned his over. "Look at this!"

Buddy flipped his coin backside up. "Wow!" He rubbed the surface of the letters. Their names were printed respectively and curved around a full blazing sun. "Thank you, Mr. Mulligan."

"Yeah," said Charlie. "They're worth more than quarters now."

"It's the value of your youth, my friends."

He adjusted his hat back over his long white hair. "They will keep you both together until you are men."

The boys looked at each other, Charlie whispered, "How did he know?"

I know everything there is to know about the folks I set out to help." Mr. Mulligan laughed. "I have to–it's part of the job." He turned around and closed up his bag. The moon-face winked.

Charlie flipped his coin over and over several times just to be sure it was real.

Buddy rubbed his quarter between his fingers.

"Okay, boys." Mr. Mulligan spoke in a loud, excited voice. "Put the coins in your pockets, the show is about to start." He set the valise on the dirty, wooden floor.

"Are we going back?" Buddy stared up at the man of magic.

"We're sure gonna give it an honest try." He braced himself against the jolting of the train. "Let's get you lads back in place."

The boys started climbing the containers on the opposite end of the boxcar. Charlie made it up first. Mr. Mulligan lifted Buddy over the top, just as he had before.

"Thank you, Mr. Mulligan," said Charlie. "I didn't mean to be a smart-mouth."

Their new friend winked at Buddy and ruffled Charlie's blond hair. "If you never make a mistake, son, you never learn." I would guess that's what this whole day's been about." He adjusted his top-hat and smiled. "Here we go."

Buddy lay flat and swallowed hard. His heart thudded.

Charlie leaned over the edge of the cartons and stared.

William Jonathan Mulligan stood in the center of the rolling railroad car and raised his arms high above his head. "Workers of magic, guardians of the universe, hear the plea of a humble servant." The would-be wizard reached higher and spread his fingers wide. He blinked his radiant eyes and continued. "Return this time and space to an instant past. The lesson has been taught. Its message will last."

The rumble and shake of the boxcar became violent.

The boys hung on with all their strength and stared, wide-eyed, through pale faces of fear.

"Might of the stars." Mr. Mulligan's voice rose against the wind. "Power of the sun, come together as one." He shouted against the rising thunder. "Carry us back to a time that has been– the boys will remain boys until it's time to be men."

The raging wind drove the big man's clothes fast against his unyielding frame. It shook them into baggy waves of cloth. His hat flew against the opposite wall of the boxcar. His silver hair danced and twisted at the roots. Gray dust spun around the magic man like fine, dry snow.

Shaking-clatter and speed grew.

A sight he was, this magic-man–like the head of a storm himself.

"He can't do it alone." Buddy shouted into the fury. "We believe Mr. Mulligan." He reached over and shook Charlie. "Say it!"

Charlie hung on and stared into the storm below.

"Tell him, Charlie." He punched the older boy on the arm. "C'mon–you gotta say it!" He walloped his friend again.

"Okay–okay!"

Charlie snapped out of his trance. "We believe, Mr. Mulligan–we do!" He yelled as loud as he could to get his voice above the blowing and banging.

Mr. Mulligan squinted his glowing eyes into the sun. The corners of his smile turned up higher. White-blue energy crackled from his fingertips.

The pounding wrath stopped.

Silence.

The clacking, clamor and vibrating ceased.

Dense blackness filled the boxcar.

A sprinkling of bright stars appeared in the void, then disappeared.

Bright sunlight filled the center of the car.

Buddy felt a tingling cold brush across his face. "Huh?"

Charlie grabbed for his friend's arm.

Buddy whispered, "I thought I felt … nothin'."

Both boys were quiet.

The train had stopped.

Footsteps on the cinders came closer.

A rough looking railroad man came up to the open boxcar door. "They're here all right."

Another man jumped into the car looking mean and mad. "What are you kids trying to do, get yourself locked in here?"

"No, sir," defended Charlie. "We just wanted to take a ride." He grabbed a short breath. "We got locked in at Jefferson Station." He started to climb down off the cartons.

Buddy followed.

"You're at Jefferson Station, boy and your young butts are in bad trouble!" He took off his ball-cap and slapped it hard against his leg. "If that old bum hadn't seen you kids, you'd be on a long train ride and you'd be locked in for who knows how long."

"Mr. Mulligan?" Buddy stared at the unpleasant man.

"A baggy old tramp with a suitcase. He saw you climb in here just before we were ready to shut and lock the doors." He slapped his hat across Buddy's backside. "Now, get outta here!"

"Run!" Charlie grabbed Buddy's arm.

The boys jumped off the boxcar and ran like the wind.

They shot between train cars, around stacks of crossties, past tool sheds and in behind a row of shuttered warehouses.

"They chasing us?" Buddy's lungs were about to burst.

"Hell no–we lost em' right off." Charlie eased himself down on a set of cement steps, and sat back. "Whoa … what a Saturday."

The younger boy leaned on the steps next to his friend. "Charlie?"

"Yeah?" He was trying to catch his breath. "What?"

"We can't tell anybody about what happened." He wiped a lock of hair from his sweaty face. "Nobody."

"Are you nuts?" Charlie ran his sleeve across his brow. "You say one word about today and we'll be laughed at for a year." He got to his feet. "How much money you got? I want a hotdog or something."

They dug their soiled hands into dirty pockets and brought out several coins.

Charlie said, "God, I forgot." He pulled out the special quarter.

"I did too." Buddy looked at his hand full of coins.

Each boy stared at his moon-faced silver quarter and wondered.

A sudden gust of wind blew up a funnel of dust, dried leaves and twigs. It spun in place for a moment, then moved off between buildings and dissipated.

The echo of a deep, warm laugh bounced off the painted bricks of the lonely warehouse.

Keep the coins, my friends, they should not be spent. They are the value of your friendship and the treasure of your youth.

Buddy looked up and pointed. "What's that?"

A shadow moved on the brick wall. In a moment it was gone.

Charlie admired his coin again. "Look!"

Buddy examined his special quarter. "Wow!"

The smiling quarter moon on each one winked.

* * * *

Author Notes:

My story is fiction, of course, but the tale of two boys getting locked in a boxcar is true. The kids, thirteen and fourteen, hopped an outbound train from a rail yard just inside the south western tip of Wisconsin. They rode the train a few miles to its next stop.

The boxcar they were in was, in fact, loaded with cases of beer bottles that still had some brew in them. The train was headed for a brewery in Milwaukee where the car would be set out on a siding.

The boys were drinking the stale beer and having a great time. Both doors of the boxcar were open and the kids could get off anytime. The train stopped in a switching yard. The kids couldn't get out without getting caught so they hid on top of the cases. Railroad workers came up quickly, closed and sealed the doors.

The boys said later that they had yelled, but there was so much noise they weren't heard.

Two weeks later, mostly dehydrated, weak and sick, the boys were rescued. A switching crew heard banging coming from inside the boxcar.

The two kids survived by drinking the stale beer. Authorities said if not for the calories in the brew, the boys would have died.

Both kids swore they actually ate pieces of cardboard torn off from the cases.

I read the story in a newspaper and it planted the seeds for my fictional tale.

Ted

Call me Jen

"*K*nock–knock."

"Come in."

"I got a message you wanted to see me."

"Please sit down, Ms. Harper."

"Already, I don't like your expression or the tone of your voice."

"Is there something you didn't understand about the assignment?"

"You wanted a four page story with believable dialogue exchanges. That's exactly what I handed in."

"Jennifer, didn't you see the words, dialogue only?"

"Yes, I did, Larry—"

"Excuse me, it's Professor Thomas."

"You just called me by my first name."

"My apology. Now, back to your story."

"You address me as Jennifer in class, why not here in your office?"

"There are twenty-seven other students in the lecture hall. I like a relaxed, friendly atmosphere when I'm teaching."

"Aren't you teaching now?"

"Yes, I am, but we're alone in my office and it would be inappropriate for us to get friendly. I'm sorry I used your first name."

"I agree. It wouldn't be appropriate."

"Then we need to discuss your work. That's the reason I wanted you to come in."

"Okay, but I'm afraid of what you might do with it."

"I don't understand that. There's nothing to be afraid of, I assure you."

"The MFA is important to me, Professor."

"I know it is, and I want to help you get it, but you're going to have to earn it."

"I'm really trying, but I just can't do it right."

"All you have to do is remove the narrative, the he-said-she-said and it will become the assignment I asked for."

"That's it and I'll pass?"

"Do what I've suggested and I'll raise your grade. You need to pass this semester or you won't get your MFA. Do the work and I'll help you."

"Am I really qualified to be a novelist?"

"Yes, I actually think you are."

"Professor, your segment of the program is a make it or break it for my MFA. I appreciate your extra help."

"I've always liked your work. You've sidestepped a lot. Sometimes that can be a good thing. Do what I require, and I promise, you'll get your MFA."

"It's in the bag, Larry."

"I don't understand."

"I've recorded this entire session with you. Every question I asked, you answered perfectly. Each statement you made has been documented on tape."

"What are you talking about?"

"I anticipated your responses and they were perfect."

"Why would you do such a thing?"

"The degree, Professor—I want the MFA!"

"Ms. Harper, what the hell are you trying to do?"

"It's done, Larry. I have a friend in an off-campus sophisticated, state-of-the-art audio lab. He will edit everything you've said to me into a polished version of this rough draft from what I wanted you to say. I took the liberty of typing it out ahead of time. Here's a copy for you."

"Why would you do this to me?"

"Don't feel exclusive. I've made it work with three other professors in the program and not a single one will ever say one tiny little word."

"You could just earn your MFA."

"That's a lot of hard work, Larry. I prefer to skate along."

"You won't get away with this bullshit!"

"I already have. You pitch a bitch to administration or the Dean and they'll all be listening to a pristine copy of the recording and reading a transcript of the document."

"You're not worthy of this program! I'm turning you in."

"I don't think you'll care to risk your reputation and tenure on what the media would do with this."

"Get out of my office right now. I want you out of here!"

"Easy, Professor, you've just dropped in another gem. *I want you.* That'll work well on the edited tape."

"You'll be thrown off this campus."

"I doubt it. You did teach me well. I learned how to turn a phrase and make dialogue count. I'm quite pleased with that."

"I'm calling security."

"You don't really want to do that, Larry. Take a minute and read along with me. I think you'll get a kick out of how I structured this dialogue sequence. I should get an A-plus for the way I did it."

"You're impossible."

"Not really, just smart. Read along with me, Larry. Here's a rough draft of what I'll put together in the final piece."

There's nothing to be afraid of, I assure you. Do what I've suggested and I'll raise your grade. You're going to have to earn it.

Am I really qualified to be a novelist?

Yes, I actually think you are. I've always liked you, I want you, Jennifer. Do what I require and I promise, you'll get your MFA.

"Nice, huh, Larry? Good work on dialogue?"

"You can't do this!"

"It's a done deal, Professor."

"I'll fight you."

"I don't really think so. You can try, but think about the wife and kids, Larry. You don't want any part of this friendly session going public do you?"

"You bitch!"

"You can call me, Jen."

Sally's Grave

*D*onna broke away a small portion of cold bun and chewed it thoughtfully.

"I didn't mean to upset you," Rachel said. She had just described being attacked behind Brandywine Elementary in detail.

"No, it's all right. I need a minute to let it sink in." She glanced at Rachel and then looked away. "My son truly believes the Perkins boy was responsible for Sally's death. You know that?"

"Yes." She thought a moment, measuring her words. "He believes Arty did it. I heard him say so."

Donna tore off another piece of bun, put it in her mouth, and stared out through the curtained windows. After a long moment she whispered, "Did he tell you about the accident?"

Rachel took a sip of coffee. "Yes. He spoke about it in detail."

"I saw Pauly through all of that. God, it was painful for him. What a horrible thing for a little boy to deal with."

Again, considering each word before she spoke, Rachel said, "The way he tells it … it wasn't really an accident."

Silence.

After another bite of hot cross bun, Donna nodded. "I never thought it was an accident, but I couldn't accept what that meant."

The waitress brought fresh coffee and offered to warm the rolls. Rachel said yes and ordered two more from the oven. When they were alone again, she said, "You're aware of Pauly's visions?"

Donna added cream to her coffee and stirred it. Hearing someone else put words to her son's problems troubled her. She looked at Rachel, and then into her cup.

"Something's been wrong for years. When Pauly was in the army, his letters were strange. On occasion, he said he'd heard from Sally. That scared me. If I asked him about it in a return letter, he'd say it was just a dream." Donna sipped her coffee. "Did he tell you about any of this?"

"Not exactly. I think it was a slip. The most he said came out in yesterday's rage."

For a moment, Donna was silent and fought tears. "I told you I heard him talking to Maribeth." Her words were slow and even. "He's been talking to Sally for nearly fifteen years." Her voice cracked. She swallowed hard and sighed. "Sorry. I've never said it out loud before."

Rachel reached across the table and patted her hand. "I understand how you feel. I love Pauly. I need to know how to deal with him in this, and I thought we might be able to help each other." She smiled. "If it's too difficult for you, we don't have to talk about it."

"No, please … I'm glad I can share it. I've held it in so long." She blinked rapidly and looked away. "I ached for him every time he had one of his spells."

"Spells?"

"Yes. I told myself they were spells because the only time he talks to Sally is when he's having a migraine."

The waitress returned with their reheated hot cross buns. "Here we are. More coffee?"

"Please." Both women spoke at the same time. They laughed. The waitress poured and left.

"Yesterday, when Pauly was so upset he kept pressing his temples, I could almost see the throbbing in his eyes. I didn't know what to make of it. The episode scared the hell out of me,"

"The headaches started after Sally's funeral. Then they seemed to go away."

"Did you take him to a doctor?" Rachel sliced her roll in half and buttered it.

"Yes. He said the migraines were caused by the boy's deep emotional upset. Nightmares too. They came frequently." She relaxed and began eating her bun.

"Pauly's had bad, really dark dreams when he's been with me." She studied the table as she said it and blushed.

Donna grinned. "Don't be embarrassed, you're both over twenty-one. I know how times have changed."

"Thank you. You're a lot like my mom." Rachel's uneasiness left her.

"I'd like to meet your parents."

"Really? We're Jewish." She felt her cheeks getting hot again.

Donna laughed. "So, we're Catholic. That would make an interesting wedding."

"Wedding," Rachel whispered as a whole ceremony flashed in her mind. "You know, with Pauly, I think it could be possible. I'm telling the truth when I say I've never had these feelings about anyone else."

"My son has changed for the better since he's been seeing you. I pray he can change for good."

"Did you ever hear Pauly talking in his nightmares?"

"Sometimes he would mumble about Sally and Arty. That didn't bother me so much because bad dreams were expected after what he'd gone through. What really scared me were the wide-awake nightmares."

"Awake?"

Donna spread a pat of butter on the second half of her roll. "It started when his headaches got worse. He was about twelve." She put her hand to her mouth. "My Lord," she whispered. "It just now occurred to me."

"What is it?" Rachel wiped her mouth with her napkin and took a sip of coffee. She didn't want things to get any stranger than they already were, but she knew in her heart that would be the case.

"Pauly's crush on Maribeth and the wide-awake dreams came at the same time. That's when I first heard him talking to Sally. His migraines got worse too." Donna sliced her bun in two.

"He doesn't know you heard him?"

"No. When he'd have a spell, he'd go to his room, turn out the lights, and lie in the dark. The doctor told him it would help." She took a small bite of her roll. "I didn't want him taking too many pills, but sometimes they were his only help." She finished her coffee. "I felt so sorry for the boy. Some of his headaches were so bad he'd have to go in the bathroom and vomit. Sorry."

"It's all right. I want to know what Pauly's been through. I wish I'd known all this yesterday when he had that episode."

"Anyway, I'd hear him through the bedroom door. Not everything, but enough. At first, I thought he was grumbling about his throbbing head and then I heard her name, clear as a bell. Once in a while, I swear I heard him pleading with her. I know I heard him say he couldn't do that. What he meant, I have no idea. Then it stopped."

"Just like that?"

"Yes. The nightmares and his spells just ended. For a long time too."

"When did that happen?"

The recollections had shed light on Donna Wakeland's hardest year. Her husband had died, and she was a young widow in deep depression. A sliver of old pain pricked way down in her heart. She paused a moment or two and blinked away aching tears. "Phil, my husband, had been gone less than a year when it got worse for Pauly. I guess I became more aware of my children then. Things stand out from that time."

"Oh, Donna … I'm so sorry. I didn't mean to bring all that up for you."

"It's all right, honey, really. Give me a minute."

Rachel took her hand as if doing so could somehow drain off a measure of hurt. "I am sorry," she said.

Donna drew a long shaky breath and went on. "Maribeth, Pauly, and his ever-present sister played together constantly for most of that year. Then Maribeth took up with an older boy and it was over."

"Did his spells end then?"

"He had one more real bad one. I almost went into his room when I heard him crying out to Sally, but I didn't."

"Was he angry at Maribeth?"

"I don't really know. He never said much. Penny teased him a lot, but Pauly didn't seem to be too upset. About a month later, Maribeth's new boyfriend was nearly killed."

"Killed?" Rachel whispered. "Was it an accident?"

"It was horrible. The boy and some of his friends made a game out of hopping freight trains. The paper said he fell. He could've been chopped to pieces." She shook her head. "The boy, Robert Pate, was found lying beside the track by his buddies. He had a broken arm and leg, and was frightened half to death. Robert said someone wearing a ski mask attacked him. He lost his grip and tumbled off the train."

"My God."

Donna cleared her throat and settled back. "I remember the accident specifically because Pauly's spells ended at that same time. He didn't have another one for over a year, if I'm remembering right."

"Did Pauly have any reaction to the near death of Maribeth's boyfriend?

"Not that I recall. Except for his scrapbook. He kept every newspaper story of Sally's drowning and Arty Perkins's fatal toboggan accident." She finished her coffee.

Rachel ate the last of her hot cross bun. "Pauly mentioned Arty's death." She wiped her mouth. "How did it really happen?

"In a way, it's strange ... puzzled me at the time." She hesitated. "You see, Pauly was involved and that's what was never solved."

"How was he involved?" Rachel already knew and dreadful images came to life.

"I knew Arty Perkins was a bully--a really bad boy. He picked on Pauly a lot. Thing is, Pauly was riding the toboggan with Arty, and that didn't make sense to me." She looked off toward the bright windows. "When I asked him about it, he said they were trying to be friends. Pauly was scraped and bruised and said he felt sorry for Arty."

"You said something about a scrapbook and the boy who was almost killed by a train."

"Yes, that puzzled me too." She folded her hands and looked down at them. "Pauly cut out all the newspaper accounts of the accident and pasted them in his book. He told Penny that the boy deserved what he got."

The sound of Pauly's fitful, rasping declaration echoed in Rachel's head. *I've got to kill Arty* again. A mixture of shock and fear swept through her. "Did Pauly have any other girlfriends after Maribeth?"

"Penny told me he'd taken up with a Negro girl, but I never believed it." Donna hesitated and then looked away. "I hate to admit it, but at the time, I couldn't bring myself to believe it."

"Do you think he might have been seeing that girl?"

Donna blushed. "I don't know, but during the time Penny was teasing him about it, he had more spells."

Rachel shook her head. "Dear God … his episodes seem connected to relationships almost every time."

"I know, and it scares me to death. Something else bothers me too."

"Tell me."

The waitress came up to the table. "Everything all right here?"

"May I have more coffee?" Donna asked.

Rachel shook her head. "None for me thanks." They were silent until she left.

"Between Maribeth and the Negro girl, if there ever was one, Pauly spent a lot of time visiting Sally's grave."

Rachel shifted her eyes around the café and focused on the huge stone fireplace built into the far wall. A bright pine log fire crackled, and the atmosphere felt warm and normal. She saw herself snuggled with Pauly on a blanket in front of the wide hearth, an image far removed from his anger and pain.

Donna patted Rachel's hand. "You all right, dear?"

"Yes … I was just wondering about when he was a small boy."

"There couldn't have been a nicer, more sensitive boy in the world." Donna took a breath. "That's the way he was and why he so loved Sally. Pauly always minded and applied himself to his lessons."

"Please believe my concern is with Pauly."

"I'm sure it is, and I love you for it."
Rachel swallowed hard and looked Donna in the eyes.

"What is it, honey?"
"I want to see Sally's grave. Will you take me there?"

"Oh, my …."

Donna considered the request, remembering the agony her son endured all those years ago. She hadn't been to the grave since the funeral, and the thought of such a visit triggered memories of a long ago time when her family was whole, with a core of inner strength. Those times were buried, just as Sally was. "Yes, I'll take you to the cemetery."

They left the café in silence, each lost in private thoughts.

* * * *

The Cemetery

*R*achel drove under the ornate stone arch into the sacred area for the dead. "You're sure you don't mind coming here?"

"Not at all." Donna cleared her throat. "I feel ashamed to admit it, but I haven't been here since the poor child was buried." She had never known Sally. Her only feelings for the girl came second-hand from her son.

"Why should you be ashamed?"

"I really can't say. It's because of Pauly, I guess. This little girl had a profound effect on my boy's life. I don't know. I suppose I should've thought more about visiting. I'm not sure. I just don't know."

"Bear with me. I don't understand why I wanted to come here either. Something just drew me." She chuckled. "Whatever it was, it worked. We're here.

The caretaker, an old man with a

cheerful smile and respectful attitude, directed them to Sally's plot. They parked nearby and walked in silence to the grave.

"Fresh flowers? Who does that, her parents?" Rachel asked.

"They moved. Wisconsin, I think. The cemetery provides perpetual care."

"It's so lonely here. Can you feel it?"

"Yes." Donna shook her head. "I can remember seeing the child alive. She was so full of life."

Rachel grabbed the older woman's arm. "Call me crazy, but I feel a presence here."

"Oh, my …."

"Maybe it's because I've shared some of this with your son. I can feel Sally—damn."

A gust of wind rustled the maple behind them, and its naked branches clacked together.

Donna bent down and arranged the bright, yellow mums.

"Pauly came here often. I know he did." She smiled. "He said he was going to the movies, but I know he came here. He spent his movie money on fresh flowers for Sally."

Crisp dry snow blew against Sally's headstone with a hissing sound that sent a rolling shiver through Rachel. She heard the sound as words—words that came from a distance. Words she felt more than heard.

Pauly will be yours when he sets me free

"Sally?" Rachel looked from side to

side, trying to see where the voice had come from.

"You called her name?"

"Yes. Let's go, I'm getting the creeps."

They left Sally's grave and the wind stopped.

From the flaming depths of hell the beast rides a black horse. In its skeletal hand, the beast holds a sword forged from the suffering and pain of condemned souls. It wears the shroud of the angel of death.

The Book of Dark Shadows

The Feeding

"Six-five to Munising dispatch, over."

"Morning, Ben, how's your Friday?"

"Great so far. I'm gassing up at Pepper's and then heading to Grand Marais to check on the incoming hunters."

"Come Monday and the woods will be a war zone."

"It's the same every year. I need to make sure all our armed visitors are legal."

"Copy that. The game warden won't be there until Sunday night."

" Who'd we draw this season?"

"Mr. Roy Clayton."

"He's new. I'm going to miss old Corey."

"Yeah, Frank's enjoying his retirement."

"Okay, Gary, I'll check in when I get to town. I think Mr. Clayton will need a little local education."

"That's a ten-four. Have a good day."

"Six-five out."

Michigan State Trooper, Sergeant Benjamin Wallace drove up to the pumps at Pepper's Shell and blew the horn on his cruiser.

No response.

Ben got out and went to the front door. It was locked. He shaded his eyes and looked through the window.

Alex wasn't inside.

Ben stepped back and knocked. "Alex."

No answer.

"What the hell's going on?"

Trooper Wallace walked around back and saw Alex's Dodge pickup. He shouted, "Alex."

Nothing.

"This is odd."

Ben got back in his patrol car and drove up to the house above the station. Alex's brother lived there alone.

When he pulled into the driveway he saw Alex sitting on the front steps with a rifle across his knees. He got out and approached the man.

"What's wrong Alex?"

When he got closer, Ben saw blood all over the front of Alex's shirt. "What happened?"

"My brother's dead—his head got taken off!"

"Did you shoot him?"

"Christ no … yeah, we fought a lot, but it never amounted to nothin' anyway."

Ben noticed the front door standing wide open. "Is Tommy in the house?"

"What there is left of him is scattered all over the living room with everything else."

"I need you to lean that ought-six against the porch, then we'll get a look inside."

"Me an' the gun are takin' after the animal that killed my brother." He stood and propped the rifle by the stoop. "You go on in, ain't no way I'm comin' with you."

Officer Wallace picked up the gun. "I'll hang on to this for now."

"You believe I'd shoot you?"

"I don't want to think that, but I see an armed man covered with blood and there's a dead body inside. You're a person of interest until I find out what's going on." He unloaded the weapon and pocketed the shells. "Turn around and put your hands behind your back."

"Ben, I ain't done nothin' at all."

"I have no choice right now."

"If you wasn't a cop, I'd be punchin' your lights out."

"This is one hell of a way to start a Friday. I'm putting you in the back of my car until I get a handle on what happened here."

"You'll damn well find out I didn't do it."

"I sure hope that's the case."

Ten minutes later, Ben came out on the porch and leaned on the railing for a moment. He shook his head and walked to the cruiser. "I'm sorry, Alex … step out of the car."

"Did you get a good look?"

"No human killed your brother."

"Didn't I tell you that?"

"I had to see for myself. Turn around." He un-cuffed Alex. "I have to call this in."

"Give me my shells, I'm going after whatever animal tore Tommy apart."

"I haven't seen the dog. Did it get him too?"

"Cesar was gone when I got here. He might be chasin' after what killed my brother."

"Let's hope he doesn't find it. The best thing you can do is go down, open the store and stay put until we're sure of something."

"It's gotta be a rogue bear—what the hell else could it be?"

"We'll find out, hopefully before someone else gets hurt, or killed."

"Can I have my ought-six?"

"It's on the porch. Now go clean up, change your shirt and open the station. I'll see that Tommy's taken care of."

"Thanks, Ben."

"I'm sorry about the cuffs."

"Yeah, me too."

Officer Wallace keyed the radio. "Six-five to dispatch, over."

"You check those hunters yet?"

"We have a bigger problem."

"What is it?"

"Tommy Pepper's been killed."

"How?" What happened?"

"I think we have a crazed bear on our hands."

"In the Seney area? Jesus, a bear attack?"

"Looks like it. Tom's been mutilated to the extreme. His left leg and right arm are missing and he's been decapitated. The man's torso is ripped wind open. I've never seen such carnage."

"God almighty—what about Alex?"

"He's stable for the moment, but he's threatened to go after the bear on his own. Tommy's dog is missing and I suspect he's tracking the bear. Contact the coroner in Newberry and I'll hold the fort until he gets here."

"Welcome to Friday."

"Tell me about it."

"I'll send the coroner right away."

"Copy that. Six-five out." Ben stared at the house with a clear image of what was inside.

* * * *

EARLIER THAT SAME MORNING:

Cesar, Tom Pepper's black Labrador followed the pungent scent of the thing that had torn his master to death.

When the dog crossed the clearing he came up on the edge of a marsh deep into the forest. Cesar caught an image in his sharp eyes. He moved forward one silent step at a time. He curled his lips back, growled and began barking.

The thing turned and looked at the dog through red eyes.

Cesar lunged forward, teeth bared.

In an instant the dog's head was torn off and his twitching body splashed into the shallow marsh.

* * * *

THREE HOURS LATER:

Sid Moran, a logging truck driver, was rolling south on M-77 with a full load. He sang along with Marty Robbins on the radio about the West Texas town of El Paso.

He down-shifted and hit the air breaks.

"What the hell!"

A late model Pontiac was stopped half across the road.

Sid climbed out of the cab of the Mack ready to read the riot act to the driver. He approached the car and stopped short. "Oh my god in heaven!"

A man and woman were slumped in the front seats bathed in carnage and blood. A small poodle lay on the back seat bleeding and whimpering in pain.

The passenger door had been forced open and bent forward against the front fender.

Sid stumbled to his truck and called the dispatcher.

* * * *

Just as the coroner's two assistants carried Tom's remains out of his house Ben's radio squawked "Six-five."

"Wallace, go ahead." He had pulled the mike through the open driver's window and leaned on the roof of the cruiser.

"You still at Pepper's?"

"The coroner's people just got Tom in a bag."

"Don't let them leave. You got two more."

"What?"

"About halfway between where you are and Grand Marais a truck driver found a male and a female mauled in their car. His dispatcher told him to hold tight until you get there, over ... Ben?"

"Yeah, I heard you. Use a land line and call Sykes' Garage. Tell him to send a tow on my order and not one word about what's in the car."

"Can you get there first?"

"You can bet your ass on it and the coroner will be right behind."

"Should I send another unit down there?"

"Not yet, I'll let you know later."

"Copy that. We're clear."

The coroner was talking to his people behind the van and then started walking to his own vehicle.

Ben shouted, "Hang on, Ray. Tell your guys to follow behind you and me."

"What?"

"We got two more of the same up the road."

"Jesus."

"Yeah, right." He jumped in the patrol car and pulled out on M-77 headed north under code three.

* * * *

When the car hit eighty Ben eased off the accelerator.

The headache started.

"Shit—I don't need this now." He flew passed three cars and a pickup as the blue cruiser sped north. "This will be a three-ring circus when these people get on scene. Dammit!"

* * * *

Alex Pepper finished taking care of a Ford station wagon crammed with a family of six. "Thank you, Have a good trip an' be careful."

"We will." The young man took his

change. He and three of the four kids carried their purchases out to the wagon. As soon as they pulled away, Alex locked the front door and checked his thirty-ought-six. He bolted a round into the chamber, went out the back door and locked it. "I'm comin' after you, you son-of-a-bitch."

* * * *

"I knew it." Ben stopped his patrol car in front of the Pontiac, got out and left the lights flashing. "I want all of you away from that car. This is a crime scene. Get back in your vehicles and continue about your business."

Sid was leaning against his truck holding the poodle. "It died."

"You should've left it alone."

"I've never seen anything like this in my life."

"Neither have I."

The cars Ben had passed were arriving and stopping in the northbound lane. "Keep it moving folks, there's nothing to see here."

"What happened, officer?" The man driving a pickup was clad in hunting clothes.

"I said keep it moving, you're blocking traffic." He waved at the line of cars. To Sid he said, "I need your help right now. Put the dog back in the car and direct these tourists around the scene."

"Okay, sure." He took the dead puppy to

the car and laid it on the back seat.

Two young men walked up on the passenger side of the Pontiac. "Holy shit. Look at that."

Ben snapped around. "Get the hell away from there and take your asses out of here. Now!"

"Yes, sir."

"Move!"

The coroner pulled onto the shoulder of the southbound lane and the van came up behind him.

"Sid, direct these people around this mess until the tow gets here."

"I'm on it."

The coroner looked in the front seat of the victim's car. "Good God."

Officer Wallace leaned on the roof of the car. "Have your men pull wallets from the man and the woman's purse so I can get ID. I'll run the license plate."

"This isn't any crime, Ben. We got a raging bear on our hands."

"My thought at first, but what bear rips open a car door and bends it around the front fender?"

"God only knows."

"Yeah, I guess." His Ray-Bands were dark, but they weren't doing their job. The bright sunlight pushed through and the migraine continued.

Ten minutes later the coroner handed Ben two wallets. "Thanks, Ray. This is the hardest part. I'm waiting for confirmation on the Plate."

"We'll take the bodies down to Newberry with Tom. I wish I could say, have a great day, but I don't think that's going to be the case."

"You got that right."

Jess Marks pulled up in his tow truck. And got out. "Hi, Ben, what've we got here?"

"A car that needs towing."

"Okay, no problem."

"Take it back to the garage, put it inside and tell your boss not to let anybody near it."

"What's the big deal?"

"The whole thing is the big deal, are we clear?"

"Yeah, I get the picture, but everybody knows something's up"

"Just make sure you don't spill any more beans."

"Hey, I hear you."

"Good." He addressed Sid. "Hold traffic until Jess gets this car out of here."

"You got it."

Ben slid into his cruiser and keyed the radio. "Six-five to Munising dispatch, over."

"What is it Ben?"

"Do you have confirmation on the victim's ID?"

"That's a ten-four. The Pontiac is registered to a Mr. Dan Goodman in Lansing at 1201 Parker Lane."

"Thanks, it's a match. Notify next of kin. I

hate this part of it."

"So do I. Sorry you're having a bad Friday."

"Yeah, Six-five clear."

Ben sat in his cruiser and watched Jess pull the death car off the road and tow it back toward Grand Marais. He opened the glove box and got his medication. Those pills would be with him for the rest of his life. There were two left and they went down with a swallow of cold coffee.

They'll have to do for today I guess. He put the bottle away and keyed the mike. "Six-five, over."

"Go ahead, Ben."

"The scene is clear and the vehicle is on its way to Sykes' Garage."

"Any problems?"

"I had to chase off a swarm of rubbernecks and a few got a good look at the mess."

"Not good. The media will be all over it."

"Keep a lid on it, Jimmy. If they call, tell them it was a fatal car accident. No reporter is going to drive up here for that."

"Was it like the incident at Tom's place?"

"Worse, I haven't seen such carnage in a decade."

"Copy that. Are you headed up to town?"

"I'll be on the way in a minute. If whatever this animal is and isn't nailed by Sunday, the game warden will have to postpone deer season."

"You're in for a tough call there, Ben."

"You got that right. Six-five out."

"Good luck. We're clear."

Ben fired up the Crown Vic and left his lights flashing in code two.

Within a few minutes he caught up to the tow truck and shot around it at seventy five. The sight of the Pontiac sent a shiver up his left arm.

The pills had eased his headache, but the medicine had no effect on the memory of the horror that ended his Air Force career ten years earlier.

* * * *

USAF INFERMERY
NORTHEN NEVADA
BUILDING 24 – RM 387
SECURITY LEVEL RED

"Captain Wallace, can you respond?"

The voice sounded distant. Ben opened his eyes to blurred images of two people in white. He tried to sit up. The pain in his left arm forced him back down. "Where is it?"

"It's over, Ben, you're in intensive care."

His vision started to clear. A mental flash of angry red eyes and sharp claws made him shudder. "Where the hell is it?"

"They caught it, Captain. Thanks to you, two lives were saved."

"I saw Greg's leg torn off and Liz trying to

get out of the lab."

"I'm sorry, they didn't make it, but the other two researchers got away because you held it off."

"Greg and Liz were killed?"

"I'm so sorry."

"Sorry—you're sorry? What in God's name is going on in that lab?"

"You were cleared to know what they're doing."

"Yeah, with a few chimps and spider monkeys—not some beast eight feet tall and close to three-hundred pounds. That I didn't know."

"And you're going to forget you know anything more than that."

"Who the hell are you?"

"I'm Major Charles Benson and in charge of *Project Nine.* It's a government secret you will keep for the rest of your life."

"If I don't?"

"You will not enjoy the consequences."

Ben looked at the other person. "Who are you?"

"Doctor Joan Taylor. I performed the surgery procedure on your arm."

Ben tried to raise his left arm. "Shit!" The pain was intense.

"You'll have discomfort and pain for about a year, then the arm will be as good as new. The injuries required reconstructive surgery, but it will heal and come back to full strength."

Major Benson said, "You're going to be discharged with full benefits just as if you served thirty years."

"Great ... with a bad arm."

"None of that will be in your record. You've been a security officer for eight years. If you choose to go into law enforcement, which I think you might, you'll have a clean slate."

"Thanks a hell of a lot."

Dr. Taylor said, "You will have government-provided medication for life and nobody else will know it, and that's another secret you have to keep."

"What's all this secret crap?"

Major Benson grinned. "Let's just say it involves national security. Are we clear on that?"

"Should we be?"

"Yes, Ben, I think we really should be."

* * * *

Officer Wallace shook off the memory and pulled up to the gas pumps at Sykes' Garage.

Tim came hustling up to the patrol car wiping his hands on the blue shop rag. "Did Jess get everything done right?"

"He's a couple of miles behind with the car in tow. You need to get the vehicle in one of your bays. Cover it and don't let anyone near it."

"What've we got on our hands, Ben?"

"A hell of a lot more than we need. Can you

fill the cruiser for me?"

"Sure thing."

"Will it be okay here for about fifteen minutes?"

"Can't see why not."

"Is Mayor Morris at his restaurant?"

"He was when I had breakfast there."

* * * *

Ben crossed the street and entered the *Kosey Korner*. Sheldon was chatting with a hunter seated at the counter. He saw the officer come in. "Excuse me." He waved and pointed to a booth in the back.

The trooper nodded and slid into the seat.

Mayor Morris joined him. "I hear we have a situation."

"What have you heard?"

"Alex Pepper called and told me about his brother being mauled to death by a rogue bear and said he was going after it."

"Sonofabitch—that's just what I don't need."

"That's not all. Two hunters came in about an hour ago and were talking about two bodies in a car down the road that were hauled away by the corner."

"Both stories are true and I need your help."

"What can I do?"

"Keep the hunters out of the forest."

"That's impossible, Ben. My hotel is full and they've booked my range to sight in their rifles."

"Close the range!"

"That'll cost me a lot of money."

"I don't care what it costs. Nobody goes up there, and I mean it. The range is off limits until further notice."

"They've already paid."

"Hold them off until Monday. The Game Warden will be here Sunday. If the bear hasn't been caught by then, he will postpone the opening of deer season."

"Are you nuts? You can't do that."

"I can and I will—count on it."

"I already have a cabin on Sable Lake rented out. A couple from Detroit has it for two weeks."

"What's the number?"

"It's cabin number 26 on the south shore of the lake."

"Who are they?"

"Robert and Carol Bell."

"What's the direct access road?"

"Take logging road 286 to 275, turn right. The cabin's on the hill above the lake. It's the best one I have."

"I'm sorry to have to do this, but I have to get them out of there."

"And you plan to get this crazed bear on

your own, I guess."

"It's not a bear, Sheldon."

"What then?"

"Something you never want to see in your life."

"I'm not following you."

"Trust me and shut off your cash register for a couple of days. The Game Warden won't be here until Sunday night and we can't wait that long. You and I will set up hunting parties of two men each this afternoon."

"By the time we get organized it'll be too late to start the hunt."

Ben checked his watch. "It's eleven forty five. You're right. Dawn tomorrow will have to do. Maybe Alex will find the beast and save us a lot of trouble."

"Beast?"

"Exactly—do I have your help?"

The Mayor nodded. "Absolutely."

"Good, I'm going to visit Mr. and Mrs. Bell. In the meantime, get the hunters together at the town hall."

"And I tell them what?"

"Say they're being asked to bring down a wild bear. I would guess most of them already know something about it anyway."

"I'll call Patty's diner. She's got a bunch staying in her motel."

"Good. I'm calling for assistance. When I get back from the lake I'll see you at the hall and give you a hand with the teams."

* * * *

Trooper Wallace drove Northwest along the logging road and keyed the radio. "Six-five."

"Go ahead, Ben."

"I need assistance up here."

"Right away?"

"By daybreak tomorrow."

"Copy that. How many?"

"Three units. Can you spare them?"

"Hang on."

Ben gripped the wheel with his left hand and swung a sharp right to avoid a dead deer road. "Dammit!"

A sharp, hot pain shot up the arm and pricked needles into his neck. "Jesus!"

His vision blurred.

"That's a ten-four, Ben. You'll have your backup five AM sharp."

"Thanks, Jimmy. Six-five clear." He stopped the car and grabbed his arm. The headache started. "Shit." He reached for the glove box and remembered his medication was gone. The fresh two-month supply sat on the dresser in his Munising apartment.

Ben got out of the cruiser to check the dead animal. "Good Christ—no bear did this."

An image of the red-eyed creature from the lab crossed his mind. *The deer had been terrified.*

The eight point buck had its throat ripped open, it was gutted and part of the animal's left rear quarter had been eaten away.

"I can't believe this." He felt the deer. *Ice cold, coagulated blood. The buck was slaughtered early this morning, I'd bet on it.*

He went back the car. "I need to get the Bells out of here." *If it isn't too late.*

* * * *

Night comes late to Upper Michigan because of the Northern exposure. Alex Pepper arrived at the town hall just before dark. He entered the crowded room carrying his loaded thirty-ought-six and found the Mayor talking to a group of hunters.

"Sheldon, I hear tell you're puttin' together huntin' parties."

"That we are, and you're welcome to join in."

"I know more of the woods here than any of these damn city slickers."

"You do and we could use your help."

"Who's headin' up this mess?"

"Ben and me."

"I don't see him."

"He went up to the lake to warn a couple staying in one of my cabins."

"When?"

"About noon and he hasn't come back."

"Shit. I'm goin' after him."

"He probably had police business to tend to."

"Cuts no ice—I'm goin."

* * * *

Twenty five minutes later, Alex pulled his pickup in behind Ben's patrol car. "What the hell?" He switched on all the roof lights, grabbed his high intensity flash light and got out. He checked the cruiser.

Empty. No sign of anything wrong.

He saw the dead deer. "This ain't right." He got back in the truck, drove around the animal and headed up to the lake.

* * * *

About sixty yards from the lighted cabin Alex questioned his own eyesight. Could that thing be the killer bear? Not in these parts. It's too damn big. He stepped on the gas.

When he got closer he stopped and jumped out of the pickup.

All the light caught the beast's attention. It dropped the man to the floor of the porch and let out an unearthly shriek.

A woman crouched against the front of the cabin screamed and started to get up.

Alex shouted, "Stay down!" He aimed and fired. The round struck the thing low in the right shoulder. It lunged forward and came off the porch shrieking louder.

"Sonofabitch." The second shot hit high in the left chest.

The creature screeched, glared at Alex through fiery eyes and fell face down.

Alex called out, "Ma'am, are you hurt?"

"Clawed on my legs … Robert's dead." She hugged her knees and sobbed.

Alex moved closer and kept the rifle pointed at whatever it was heaped on the ground.

The beast turned over, sat up and in a hollow, guttural voice it spoke. "Kill me!"

Carol cried out and covered her face.

Stunned, Alex stepped back and fired. The bullet struck the creature in the chest and knocked it down.

"What on God's earth am I seeing" Alex witnessed a nightmare he'd never forget.

The animal began to rapidly change from the savage beast into an ape.

"Jesus, Mary an' Joseph …."

The ape evolved to a Neanderthal.

Carol stood on shaking legs to see the final evolution into the naked, bleeding body of Trooper Benjamin Wallace. "This is something from hell."

Alex whispered, "I hope you're at peace, Ben."

"Nobody will ever believe what just

happened here." Carol looked back at her dead husband and began to cry.

"C'mon, we gotta get you to the doc."

* * * *

On the way back toward town Carol's bleeding stopped. Her legs started shaking. Pain raced through her arms and a headache hit like a hammer in her skull. She stiffened and moaned.

Alex stopped at the paved road. "Are you okay?"

"I'm hungry."

"What?"

Carol glared at him through burning eyes. Her face started changing. She reached across the cab, tore out Pepper's throat and began feeding.

The Visitor

"*I* smell a skunk."

"Janet, stay back in the hallway and don't raise your voice."

"A real skunk?"

"Yes. Keep your voice down."

"Where is it, Jack?"

"In the living room."

"What?"

"In the living room."

"How did it get in?"

"I left the door open when I went out for a smoke."

"You let a skunk in the house?"

"He came in, I didn't let him in."

"How do you know it's a he?"

"I don't.

"Take it out!"

"I can't. Stop yelling."

"I want it out."

"If we scare him he'll spray or pee, whatever a skunk does."

"Get it out!"

"Calm down. He's just sniffing the sofa."

"I can't see it."

"You will. He's on the way to the kitchen."

"Oh my God–do something!"

"He's going for the trash can."

"It's looking at me. I'm going to scream!"

"Do not scare him."

"He stinks."

"Skunks stink. Can you reach the back door?"

"Yes, if I lean around the washer."

"Do it slowly and open it easy."

"I'm afraid."

"You're bigger than he is. Open the door."

"It's watching me."

"He wants out. Open the door."

"Nice skunk. Go home."

"He's leaving–you did it."

"Don't you ever, ever let another skunk in this house."

"I won't, I promise ... not even your polecat brother."

As promised, this is chapter one from my new novel, "The Legs Collector" It will be available on Amazon, B&N and other retail outlets by early to mid October, 2011.

Smooth Soft Legs

*C*old, hard rain spattered against Michael's bedroom window with wind-driven fury.

Lightning flashed in the distance.

A few seconds later a clap of thunder rattled the glass.

Each flare of white-hot electricity revealed Mickey's image in the dresser's mirror. He hated the nickname, but his mother would never call him *Michael.* She taunted him. *Mickey, Mickey, Mickey Mouse—that's who you are, and will always be! Stupid, Mickey Mouse.*

Another jagged strike reflected an image of his mother standing behind him. *You've been worthless since you were ten!*

Her scolding voice echoed in his head.

"Shut up, Mother! You're dead twelve years—leave me alone."

The next rolling thunder came sooner and covered Michael's painful scream, "Stay dead!"

He fell back on the bed and covered his eyes.

* * * *

When Mrs. Elizabeth Moran passed on, Michael inherited the fourteen room Victorian and a substantial family fortune. The old house was in good repair and Michael kept it up. After all, he worked at home.

He had just turned thirty-six-years-old, was in excellent health and completely independent.

Mickey had an obsession. He loved young women with beautiful, long legs.

* * * *

At the far end of the hospital-clean basement, Michael had built a good sized operating room. Of course, he hadn't gone to the expense required for an EKG monitor, resuscitator nor the services of an anesthetist.

No need, his patients would never feel a thing when he started cutting.

"It'll all be over soon, Mary Jane." He tied on a surgical mask, as if it mattered, scrubbed his hands, air-dried and snapped on a pair of latex gloves.

"Ready." Would-be Dr. Michael Moran smiled. "I assure you, Ms. Ott, I've spared no expense on the most precision surgical instruments available."

* * * *

CRYSTAL PIER
4500 OCEAN BLVD.
SAN DIEGO, CA
MONDAY - 7:30 AM:

Detective Ken Black squatted beside the body. "This looks like a shark attack, why call us?"

"If it is, the fish has training in surgical procedure."

Medical Examiner, Judith Wake stood, waved at the two men from the coroner's office and made a note on her clipboard. "I called you guys because the Vic has ligature marks on her neck and wrists."

Special Victims detective Matt Kellogg joined them. Any sign of sexual assault, Doc?"

"I won't know that until I get her on the table. The woman's been in the water for about four hours."

Kellogg looked at his partner. "The vic's been strangled and tied up. She had her legs cut off and was dumped under the pier. It's our case."

Ken shook his head. "Anything on cause of death?"

Dr Wake stepped aside to let the body bag crew have the corpse. "I won't know until I open her up."

Matt lit up a Pall Mall. "I hope to Christ she was dead before her legs were cut off."

* * * *

MONDAY – 8:30 AM:
FOOD COURT – GROSSMONT
SHOPPING CENTER
LA MESA, CA
STARBUCKS:

The counter girl smiled and handed Sally Patterson her usual foamy Cappuccino. "Be careful, it's hot. How was your special weekend behind the scenes at the zoo?"

"It was the most fantastic experience with animals I've ever had."

"Great! We'll have lunch and you can tell me all about it."

"I have pictures—I got to pet a cheetah!"

"Oh my God! Can we do lunch today?"

"Yes, I'll come by."

Sally beamed. "I have more good news."

"What?"

"My promotion came through at PETCO. I'll tell you about it at lunch."

"I can't wait to hear the details."

Michael sat at a small table near the front of the coffee shop and heard every word of Sally's excited conversation. She turned him on. He smiled and sipped his latté.

Beautiful, young, Ms. Patterson had no idea that deciding to wear a short skirt that Monday morning was a fatal mistake.

Michael admired the shape, form and tone of the young woman's beautiful legs. *Ms. Sally, I believe you and I are going to get to know each other.*

* * * *

SDPD – SQUADROOM – 11:30 AM
SPECIAL VICTIM'S UNIT:

Matt picked up on the second ring. "Kellogg. What've you got?" He made a note. "Thanks, we'll be right there."

Ken got up from his desk and pulled his jacket off the back of the chair. "That was Judy, right?"

"She has a COD on our vic and an ID."

"I guess we're going to the morgue."

"That's where they keep the cold ones."

"Including those without legs."

"Ken, sometimes your humor sucks."

* * * *

GROSSMONT CENTER 12:45 PM:
HOOLEYS RESTRAUNT:

Sally and her friend, Lauren, from Starbucks, were having a good time enjoying their lunch.

Michael had browsed around the PETCO store and then waited out front until he saw Sally leave. He followed her to Hooleys where she met up with her friend. The eatery was just a short walk away.

Sally's animated conversation was not difficult to hear. "You wouldn't believe what it's like behind the scenes at the zoo."

Lauren bubbled with excitement. "The cheetah—weren't you afraid?"

"Not for a second. The handler was right there. I scratched the cat's neck and he purred like a kitten, only a lot louder."

"I'm so happy for you. Does your promotion change anything?"

"Nope, I'm in at the same time, out at five-thirty and off on weekends."

Michael smiled and took a bite of his calamari taco. *I'm happy for you too, Sally. It will be so nice to have your legs.*

* * * *

KEARNEY MESA – SAN DIEGO
CITY/COUNTY MORGUE
SAME TIME:

Dr. Wake pulled the sheet down. "Your vic is, Mary Jane Ott, twenty-eight."

"COD?" Ken studied the face of the dead woman.

"It was death by strangulation. The perp used some kind of rubber tubing or a pair of pantyhose."

Matt bent down to get closer look. "Why do you say that?"

Judy drew her finger across the Vic's throat. "The ligature marks are consistent with a material that would stretch or give as it was pulled around the neck. Ordinary rope wouldn't do that, and it would've left burn marks."

"Were her wrists bound the same way?"

"No. He used some type of rope." She raised Mary Jane's left arm from under the sheet so Ken could see the difference. "The abrasions are slightly smaller and the burns are obvious."

Matt said, "May I?"

"Go ahead."

He lifted the woman's right arm and studied her wrist. "I'm wondering which was done first?"

"Does it matter?"

"It helps give me a little insight into the killer."

"Judging from the forensics, I'd have to say he tied the hands first. The bruising would be less otherwise."

Ken jotted a note. "How so, Dr.?"

"It would take time to complete the strangulation and remove the tubing or the pantyhose. The vic's heart would've stopped pumping blood when he got to the hands and ankles. I'm guessing he tied those too."

As Matt covered the woman's right arm he said, "You've called the perp *he* several times, why?"

"I saved the worst for last. There's vaginal and anal tearing and the acts were performed post mortem. He used a condom. There are no fluids to find."

Ken made another note. "This maniac is a necrophile!"

"And he's medically skilled. I said so at the crime scene. Your perp removed Ms. Ott's legs with surgical precision."

"The pier was the dump spot. The crime scene is somewhere else."

Matt took a last look at Mary Jane. "Thanks, Doc."

"Anytime, gentlemen. Tony has all the paperwork at the crime lab."

"You're a peach."

"So I've been told."

* * * *

HOOLEYS – GROSSMONT CENTER
1:30 PM:

Sally picked up the lunch check. "It's my treat to celebrate my promotion."

Lauren finished her green tea. "I'm so proud of you. It's been tough, but you did it, girl."

"Yeah … I guess, but I lost Nick in the process."

"True, but wasn't he more about *Nick* than he was about you?"

"It turned out that way."

"I don't want to be an alarmist, but there's a very attractive man two tables behind you who's been intently watching us."

"Is he's good looking?"

"Yes."

"Then there's hope yet."

"Don't turn around. There's something I don't like."

"What?"

"He's the same dude who was eyeing you at the coffee shop this morning."

"Are you sure?"

"Positive—I don't like the feel of it."

"I'm going to look."

"Don't."

She turned around.

Michael smiled.

The ladies got up and left the table.

He enjoyed every move of Sally's legs as she and Lauren walked toward the cashier.

* * * *

SDPD – CRIME LAB:

Chief investigator, Tony Gonzales, got up from his work station to greet Matt and Ken. He handed Matt a file folder. "Everything you need is in there. I ran her through the national data base she came up clean. Her prints came back as a match from DMV. Ms. Ott's address is, 6021 Severin Drive, La Mesa."

"What else did you get?"

"She needs corrective lenses to drive."

"There were no glasses where she was found and Judy didn't mention contacts." Matt sat on the edge of a work table. "Insurance information says, Mary Jane owns a late model Honda Civic. Cal plate number 5WXB097."

Tony said, "She's a donor, but that's moot, the four-hour window is closed."

Ken grinned. "I believe the Vic has already donated her legs."

The other two men stared at him.

Matt closed the folder and shook his head. "You're a sick puppy." He held up the file. "Thanks, Tony. "C'mon, numb nuts, we're headed for the La Mesa PD."

* * * *

THE OLD VICTORIAN:

Michael came up from the cellar and saw Samantha standing in the doorway. "You startled me." He nearly dropped the basket of women's clothes with Mary Jane's purse riding on top. "How many times have I told you not to sneak up on me?"

Sam's eyes were not smiling.

"I know, you want supper and I'm running late." He carried the basket down the hallway and into a large bedroom. His father had spent the last six months of his life dying there. Finally, colon cancer had claimed the poor man.

When Michael stepped into the hall, Samantha was waiting.

"You're starting to make me angry and you don't want to do that." He hesitated. "All right, c'mon, I'll fix dinner before you faint from hunger. Fat chance of that happening any time soon."

The cat swished her tail and trotted along behind.

Michael looked down at the animal. "If you're good tonight, I'll bring home one of your favorite treats."

Sam went right to her food dish, sat beside it and waited.

Michael grinned. "I believe Sally will be sweeter than Mary Jane, she has less muscle."

The gray and black cat licked her chops.

* * * *

SDPD – SQUADROOM – 4:30 PM
SPECIAL VICTIM'S UNIT:

Captain Roy Sawyer walked into the room from his office the minute the detectives returned from La Mesa. "How did it go?"

Matt went straight to his desk. He held up his notebook. "I need to make a few calls."

Detective Black opened his notepad, gestured toward his desk and walked in that direction. "Well, to start with, it's a brutal killing." He sat at his desk. "Cause of death was strangulation. She had been sodomized and there is evidence of vaginal and anal tearing."

"What the hell are we dealing with?"

"Your basic, home-grown, necrophile."

"Holy Christ. You two know the drill on that issue."

"Add to that, the perp has a thing for women with shapely legs." He hesitated. "Our vic had hers surgically removed."

Sawyer checked his watch. "Okay, this is going over the top. What do we have on the perp?"

Ken leaned back in his chair. "At the moment, we have nothing."

"Not so." Matt looked up from his desk. "The beach patrol found our vic's Honda in a parking lot near the pier. I ordered a tow."

Sawyer said, "Maybe we'll catch a break." He looked at the detectives. "Are we going to have a problem with La Mesa PD?"

"I doubt it." Ken pushed his chair up to his

desk. "Lieutenant Howard made it clear that unless the crime had been committed in his jurisdiction he doesn't want any part of it."

Matt slipped on his sport coat. "We sealed the vic's apartment after the crime team did their job. Everything was in perfect order, no sign of foul play. The complex manager told us the woman lived alone and he never saw her with anyone."

Ken put his notebook away. "Maybe it's nothing, but it struck me as odd that there are no family pictures of any kind and no next of kin. I found that out at the manager's office. The rental agreement requires a list of relatives. She checked none."

Captain Sawyer looked at his watch. "I'm not going to authorize overtime on this for now. It's past five anyway. Maybe we'll get lucky with the Honda." He paused and tapped his chin. "You two start a murder book on this case and be sure all the details are accurate. Pack it in for the night. We'll start fresh in the morning."

* * * *

THE VICTORIAN CELLAR
THIRTY MINUTES
EARLIER:

Michael stepped out of the walk-in freezer, closed the door and checked the clock. "Just an hour and half, my lovely Sally, then we meet face-to-face." He took off his white lab coat and hung it in a closet just outside the custom built operating room.

Mickey, what you're going to do is very bad.

His dead mother sat on the stainless steel operating table. "Shut up, Mother!"

You've killed innocent people, Mickey; you will have to answer for that.

He ran into the room and grabbed for the apparition. It vanished. "Stay out of my life, you old bitch!"

Michael leaned on the table and shuddered. Tears came for the first time in months. They spattered on the cold surface.

Old images played across Michael's mind.

* * * *

Two days after his father's funeral, he sat in the living room with his mother. Mrs. Moran shook her head. "I knew you'd fail the moment you were accepted in the medical program—I just knew it."

"I never wanted to be a doctor from the day Dad decided I should follow in his footsteps."

"Your father was good to you, Mickey. He died believing you were studying medicine. The poor man was proud of you without knowing you had quit."

"I didn't want to disappoint him, and he

wasn't *poor* in the least."

"No, he was not poor. Your father's surgical practice flourished. He wanted the best for you and you let him down, Mickey."

"Stop it! You know I hate that name."

"You're a failure, Mickey, a complete flop, Mickey."

"Shut up, you bitch!"

* * * *

Michael shook off the memory and looked at his watch. *Four thirty. I have an hour, no problem.*

He crossed the basement and climbed the stairs to the kitchen.

Samantha greeted him when he opened the door. "Hi, Sam." He reached down and petted the cat. "I have a date with Sally tonight. She doesn't know it yet, but she'll have the best time of her life."

Without response, the feline followed her master down the hall and into his bedroom.

* * * *

BREE APARTMENTS
EL CAJON, CA
APT 124 5:15 PM:

Detective Matt Kellogg studied the entries he had made in the murder book. He lit a smoke and sat back from his desk. "Ann, could you fix us a drink?"

"Already have, my love."

Sergeant Ann Beck brought two gin and tonics to Matt's work station. "I guess you and Ken caught a good one."

"We did and I'm going to ask the captain to put you and your partner on the case to help with the investigation."

"Fine by me and I'm sure Jack will be delighted."

* * * *

GROSSMONT CENTER
AT THE SAME TIME:

Michael waited patiently in his Mercedes. He got lucky finding a spot facing the PETCO storefront. *Don't keep me waiting, Sally.*

A moment later, Ms. Patterson appeared at one of the checkout counters and chatted with the woman on duty.

"Cut the chatter, Sally," whispered Michael. "You're wasting time." He started the car.

Ms. Patterson came out of the store and headed for the parking lot.

Michael backed out and kept Sally in sight. He watched her approach a blue Toyota. *Naughty girl. Employees are supposed to park farther away.*

He pulled up behind the Toyota and got out.

"Excuse me, I'm a little lost. Can you direct me to the Sears store?"

Sally unlocked her car and opened the driver's door. "You're in the wrong center. Sears is in Parkway Plaza in El Cajon." She took a quick breath. "You're the guy who was in Starbucks this morning."

"Very observant." He was on her before she could get in the car.

"What do you want?"

He pulled the syringe from the pocket of his leather jacket, jerked the cap off the needle and plunged it into Sally's neck. "I want your legs, your beautiful, long legs."

She struggled in his arms. "What did you do to me?" She began to go limp. "I can't see!"

"Just a temporary side effect. Don't fight the drug."

"Who are you?" Images of her co-workers and the animals in the store slipped across her mind. Lauren's face appeared and faded away. "Why are you doing this to me?" She sensed a light at the end of a long tunnel and fell toward it.

Michael held her up and put her in the front seat of his Mercedes and buckled her in. "Okay, Miss. Sally, you're safe now." He went back to the Toyota, took the keys out of the door, grabbed Sally's purse and dropped them into it. He pushed down on the door lock and closed it. I bet it'll be forty-eight to seventy-two hours before your car is found."

* * * *

BREE APARTMENTS
APT 124 6:30 PM:

Matt closed the murder book and finished bringing Ann up to speed on the Mary Jane Ott case. "I believe this crime sets a precedent for SVU."

Ann sipped her drink. "For the unit, yes it does, but not for the department."

"How so?"

"Eighteen months ago, before SVU was set up, I worked out of robbery-homicide in the north county division. Jack and I had just become partners and we caught the first of four mutilation killings."

"Right, I do remember something like that up in Rancho Bernardo. I think they called it the golf course murders."

"You're close. We labeled the case *The Oaks North File*. The victims were dumped in bushes near the maintenance building on the back nine. There were four in all. Every vic was female and the perp had surgically removed their feet."

"If memory serves, the perp is still in the wind."

"Exactly and the murders stopped. We had

several suspects, including the greens keepers, but no one had medical training or surgical skills."

"Were the victims strangled and bound?"

"Every one in the same manner as Mary Jane. And that tells me the same killer is back."

"Didn't it seem strange that all four victims were dumped in the same place?

Ann went to the kitchen to refresh her drink. "The first two had me going nuts. Then I realized what the perp was up to."

"He hated the golf course, right?"

"Actually, you're pretty close. You want another drink?"

"I'm good, thanks."

She came back from the kitchen and joined Matt at his desk. "It took a while to get a handle on it. The perp knew something about a crime scene." She stirred her drink with an index finger. "The immediate area was, of course, ground zero, but the killer knew that we'd shut down the back nine for the duration, which turned out to be ten days."

Matt pushed away from the keyboard. "That's a lot of lost revenue for Oaks North."

"Several thousand bucks a day. I believe it was the perp's intent. Two days after we ended the crime scene another footless corpse turned up in the same place. That's the way it played out with each of the victims. And they were all molested post mortem."

"I'll bet your perp and mine are the same."

"You may be right, Matt. I'll pull the cold case files in the morning and we'll go from there."

"Sounds like a plan. That's tomorrow. Right now, I'm taking you to the Red Lobster for a glutton's seafood feast."

"I think that's a great idea, Mr. Kellogg."

* * * *

THE VICTORIAN CELLAR
AT THAT SAME TIME:

The elevator doors opened into Michael's spotless basement. "Just a few minutes more, Sally and you'll be at peace forever." He pushed the wheelchair into the operating room and locked the wheels. "Just relax, you have nothing to fear."

Sally's struggle was fruitless. "What are you going to do to me?"

"For starters, I'll be enjoying your beautiful legs."

"Please don't hurt me—I've done nothing to you. I don't know you."

"Be still, you're not going to feel a thing." He lifted Sally out of the wheelchair and laid her on the stainless steel table. "Can you move your arms and legs?"

"No I can't … they're numb."

"That's a good sign. You're an excellent patient. Now I can prep you for surgery."

"Oh my God—what surgery?" Sally tried to move her arms and legs, but they wouldn't budge. "I don't need an operation. Please—don't cut me."

"You made the mistake of wearing a short skirt and exposing your beautiful long legs. You wanted them seen. You were showing off and once I saw them I had to have both all to myself."

Sally started to cry and the tears blurred her vision. "Who are you?" She managed to raise her head and see the fuzzy image of a man wearing a surgical mask. "Are you a doctor?"

"Surgeon, Sally. You might say a real specialist. My expertise is amputating lovely legs from young women who can't resist putting theirs on display."

"I'm sorry, I didn't mean to offend you."

"No offense. Actually, your legs aroused me quite a bit. That's why you flaunt them isn't it?"

"Please, let me go, I promise not to tell anyone."

"That's a nice gesture, but unnecessary. I know you won't tattle on me."

"No, I never will. Please let me go."

"I believe you, Sally." Michael picked up a three foot length of rubber tubing from a tray of surgical instruments near the operating table. "It's time for you to go to sleep."

"What are you doing?"

"Relax, in just a moment or two you'll be in heaven or hell. Of course that depends on the life you've been leading. "My guess is there's a place for you in heaven."

"Please, I haven't done anything to you."

"That doesn't matter." He put the tubing around her neck, tied a simple knot and pulled it tight. "Goodbye, Sally … rest well. Her arms and legs moved in random spasms. Her open eyes bulged and hemorrhaged internally.

"Good girl. Rest in peace." He left the ligature in place and closed Sally's eyelids. "Now, those lovely legs."

* * * *

BALBOA PARK
SAN DIEGO, CA
Tuesday 3:30 AM:

Security officer, Andy Walker came around the fountain in his golf cart and spotted someone sitting in a wheelchair in front of the Aero Space Museum. When he got closer he could see it was a woman. "Excuse me, Miss. the Park is closed, the exhibits won't be open until 10:00 AM."

No response.

Andy stopped near the wheelchair. "Did you hear me, Ma'am?"

A gust of wind blew strands of long, dark hair away from the woman's face.

"Holy Mary, Mother of Christ!"
Andy got out of the cart and approached the chair.

The woman's head had been tied to a make-shift support to appear as though she were sitting upright.

"I can't believe this." He shined his light over the corpse. The dead woman had a death grip on a blanket across her lap. Andy pulled the cover from her hands and threw it off the body. "Oh my God!" He went back to the golf cart and called it in. "Three-six to base, over."

"Go ahead, Andy."

"Get SDPD here ASAP!"

"What's the problem?"

"I have a dead woman in a wheelchair in front of the Space Center."

"What?"

"You heard me—and her legs have been cut off."

* * * *

THIRTY MINUTES LATER
BALBOA PARK
THE DROP SITE:

Detectives Kellogg and Black had joined ME, Judith Wake at the entrance to the Aero Space Museum. Ken said, "I wish this perp kept normal hours."

Dr. Wake zipped up the body bag. "The killer is on a roll and he has an agenda." She waved at the two coroner's assistants. "Take her to my lab and drop the paperwork on my desk."

"You want her in the fridge?"

"No, put her on the table and leave her in the bag."

"You got it, Doc."

"Dave."

"Yes?"

"Neither you nor your partner know anything beyond a routine body pick up. Are we clear with that?"

"Absolutely. Mum's the word."

"Great. I'll be back in my office in a couple of hours or so. Do I need to remind you that what you have in the bag can not be leaked to the media?"

"No, Ma'am, not a single word."

"Good, get her out of here."

Detective Kellogg stood by the empty wheelchair. "Ken, did you get a load of this?" He patted the right arm of the chair.

"What is it?"

He shined his flashlight where Matt was pointing. "It's a rental chair."

"Exactly, and it has a La Mesa address. Are we catching a break on this case or what?"

"Let's get some breakfast and hit East County Medical Equipment Rentals when they open. Judy, you're welcome to join us."

"You're on. I want sausage, eggs and pancakes on the side."

The Caretaker

*C*louds of dust rose into the early morning sun and turned the circling seagulls into silhouettes high above the giant yellow bulldozer.

James L. Thompson operated the huge machine with keen professional skill. The rumble of the iron beast had become a symphony to Mr. Thompson's old ears. He had turned sixty-four last June and he knew this would be the final landfill he would close for the county.

He called himself a junk man and took pride in having been so for the last twenty-five-years.

Mr. Thompson worked the levers and pedals and pushed the wide steel blade into a pile of doorless refrigerators, broken furniture, worn out tires and other discards. Each item had served a purpose in someone's life. Now they were part of another mission.

The big yellow CAT shoved the trash over the edge and it all tumbled down into the rapidly filling canyon.

He backed the dozer away from the rim of the fill and shut her down.

Squawking gulls landed on the hood of the machine cocking their heads from side to side.

"I didn't forget." The caretaker pulled off his heavy work gloves and shook a brown paper sack. "Bacon and toast this morning. I hope that meets with your approval." Several of the larger birds pushed ahead of the crowd. "I brought enough for everybody." He dumped the contents of the bag on the hood and the gulls started their breakfast. Mr. Thompson folded the bag and put it in the side pocket of his brown coveralls. He tipped his cap at his feathered friends and said, "Enjoy your meal. I'll have something more this evening." He climbed down off the dozer.

* * * *

Jim had gone halfway along the seventy-yard walk back to his office shack when he heard Davy Carter's trash truck lumbering up the entrance road. The caretaker picked up his pace and waved when the truck pulled in.

Davy swung the green and white monster around and backed toward a row of four large sheds next to Mr. Thompson's office. Jim shouted over the beeping reverse alarm, "What've you brought?"

Davy turned off the truck and jumped down from the cab. "Did you make coffee?"

"Does a bear shit in the woods?"

"Great. You'll love what I picked up this morning." He slapped an old trunk tied onto the side frame of his truck. "That's full of old books and it's heavy as hell. It'll take both of us to get it in the shed."

"Where'd you get it?"

"Two young guys brought it by the office yesterday when I was closing up. They wanted to make a dollar to recycle the paper. We don't usually take stuff like that, but I thought of you and gave them twenty bucks for it."

"I'll give you the twenty. Let's get it in the shed and take a look."

"Wait. I have something else." Davy climbed halfway into cab and brought out a small nightstand with an elaborate hand-painted flower design on the top. "I knew you'd want this." He dusted off the surface. "One of the clients on my route set it out with the trash. No charge on this, I got it free."

"Who would throw something like that away?" Mr. Thompson opened the small drawer. "It's in perfect condition. I'll bet it wasn't meant to be put out with the trash."

"It came from one of my upper crust customers over in the Ridgecrest development.

They get tired of something and toss it out without a second thought."

"Yeah, and a lot of times they regret doing so." He closed the drawer and set the stand aside. "Let's get that trunk in the shed."

* * * *

When Mr. Thompson lifted the lid on the trunk he stood back and grinned. "I can't believe it. Those young men sold this for twenty dollars?"

"They were happy to get it."

"It's a treasure chest. He picked up a book. "This is vintage Bradbury. You see this novel?"

"I'm not much for old books, but it looks like you got a lot of reading here."

"Are you kidding?" He opened the hardback and ran his finger along the inside frayed dust cover. "This is Ray Bradbury's Dandelion Wine. It's one of the original printings." He showed it to Davy. "Look at the price. It sold for three dollars and ninety-five cents."

"I wouldn't know anything about that, but I guess you do."

"Here, look at this one. " He lifted a thick volume. "A leather bound collection of Poe." Jim shook his head. "There's more Bradbury and look here." He picked up another book. "A collection of the works of Oscar Wilde."

"I'm glad I made your day."

"This is worth more than a twenty."

"I paid twenty bucks, that's all I'll take. You enjoy the books."

Mr. Thompson closed the trunk. "Nobody knowingly gives a wealth of classic literature to a recycling center. Did those guys give you an address?"

"They grabbed the money and took off."

"There's more to this. The owner of that trunk will turn up. So will the people who are involved with the discarded nightstand."

Fifteen miles across town, a shiny blue Porsche pulled up in front of 1438 Ridgecrest Drive. Civil attorney Karl Hanson got out beeped the car locked and walked to the front door.

Robert Richards answered the bell. "C'mon in, Karl," he whispered, "The battle lines have been drawn."

"Great. Just what we need before lunch."

The two men entered the vast living room. Karl nodded toward Mrs. Richards. "Morning, Cindy." He smiled at her sister. "Nice to see you, Anita."

"I can't say the same, Mr. Hanson." She took a sip from her second martini. "The way I see it, you're here to screw me out of the old man's money."

"For Christ's sake, Anita." Robert stepped away from the bar with a cup of coffee for the attorney. "Could you try to be civil for once?"

"That's his job. Isn't that right, Karl?"

"I came over to settle your father's estate just the way he wanted it."

"A little birdie told me there's a problem, counselor." Anita downed the rest of her drink and went to the bar.

Cindy gestured toward the dining room. "Let's go to the table and hear what Karl has to tell us."

Anita joined them after they were all seated. She brought a fresh martini with her. "The meeting's in session, Karl. What do you have?"

The attorney glanced at Cindy and opened his briefcase. He brought out one document and a letter. He held up the first. "This is Mr. Bartlett's original will." Karl handed the paper to Robert. "Cindy and Anita are to share equally in the entire estate. You both inherit the house, property and all liquid assets, investments and bank accounts."

Anita sat back and glared at her sister. "I deserve a hell of a lot more than half!" She emptied her glass, chewed the olive and stood. "I took care of that sick old man for the last two years of his sorry life." She stormed back to the bar. "I cleaned him up, changed his soiled sheets and put up with the creeping smell of death until it made me sick."

Robert shouted, "Shut up, Anita!"

Karl held up the letter. "Your father's will is null and void." He looked at Cindy again. "Mr. Bartlett sent me this signed document six months before he died. There's a new will."

"That's impossible." Anita dropped an olive in two jiggers of vodka and added a hint of vermouth. "Dad never mentioned that to me." She stared at the lawyer. "Do you have it, Karl?"

Mrs. Richards stood. "No, he doesn't." She went to the bar and faced her sister. "Dad didn't want you to know until after he died."

"I don't believe it, sis." She took a swallow of booze.

"Well you'd better believe it. He drew up a second will, sealed it and put it into another envelope and sealed that."

"Where the hell is it?"

"I had it certified and mailed it back to him."

"What did you do with it? I want to read it."

"I did what he wanted. I taped it on the bottom of the drawer of his nightstand." She went behind the bar and poured herself a snifter of brandy.

Anita drained her martini in one swallow. "This is really terrific, absolutely fantastic."

"What are you talking about?"

The younger woman laughed. "You should've said something, Sis. I had a cleaning crew take everything out of dear old dad's stinking sickroom and get rid of it."

"You discarded the nightstand?"

"Didn't I just say that?"

"Where did it go?"

"I don't know. It's gone, with the will."

* * * *

Mr. Thompson moved the nightstand over next to the ornate trunk and admired it for a moment. "I don't think you'll be here for too long." He rubbed his thick fingers over the flower design. "A fine piece of craftsmanship," He studied the trunk and smiled. "Somebody will want you back real soon." He locked the shed and went back to his office.

* * * *

Jim switched on his desk lamp and took a ledger from the center drawer. Every item from each of the four sheds had been listed by number and the date acquired. Mr. Thompson paged through to the last entry and added the nightstand and trunk.

* * * *

Davy's truck stopped next to the shack and let out a blast of air from its brakes. He left it idling and came into the office. "I got time for a half-cup." He took a mug from the cupboard above the coffee maker and saw Jim close the ledger. "How many is that now?"

"I have seven hundred and fifty-two pieces of usable goods." He put the ledger back in the drawer. "Pour me a cup."

"You could have a major sale up here. Ever think of that?"

"I have, but I get a kick out of giving it back to folks who thought it was lost."

Davy brought two mugs to the desk and sat in front of it. "You got a great heart, Jimmy. That's what I like most about you."

"Thank you very much."

"I'll be sad to see you go."

"Don't count me out yet. I have eight months before I'm sixty-five. Besides, I have a deal with the supervisors to stay on the job until this landfill is finished. I'm pretty sure we'll go beyond that."

"You can't count on it." He took a swallow of coffee. "I got inside word yesterday from a friend in the commissioner's office. Jarrett and Sons Sanitation and Refuse just cut a deal with the county."

"I heard they made a bid."

"It's a done deal, Jimmy." He sat back and looked at his friend. "That company is big. They have sixteen new trucks with more capacity than my five." He finished his coffee and stood. "They have three units to a route. One comes by and picks up trash, like I do. A second truck follows an hour later and collects green stuff from another barrel. The third truck picks up recycle only." He rinsed his cup and set it on a paper towel by the sink.

"That's great, Davy. There are twenty three landfills for them to feed."

"Sorry to be the one to tell you. This fill is

the target. It starts next Monday. Jarrett and Sons will be dumping here seven to ten times a day."

"I still have to push it into the canyon and level it all off. I can only do so much in a day."

"You're going to have help."

"What kind of help?"

"I wish I didn't know any of this—damn." Davy adjusted his hat. "Wednesday they're bringing in three big dozers with young operators. Between you and three more machines this fill will be closed in four months." He opened the door and turned back. "I'm sorry, Jimmy."

"Thanks. It'll all work out."

Davy hesitated. "I dumped my trash in section twenty-three."

"Good. I'll see you tomorrow."

"Yeah … take care."

* * * *

Mrs. Richards shook her head and spoke into the phone. "You're absolutely sure?" She hung up. "That's the tenth thrift store I've contacted and I've come up with zero."

Anita laughed and dropped an olive into her fifth martini. "What the hell'd you expect? You think Daddy's old nightstand is going to pop up like magic at some Goodwill store?" She sipped her drink. "It's your fault, dumb-shit. Taping a will to the bottom of a drawer was stupid. Not telling anybody is even dumber."

"Shut up, Anita—eat something, you've had too much to drink."

"What am I supposed to eat, Sis, the old dead will?"

Cindy called for the maid. "Jenny, would you come here please?"

An older woman came in from the kitchen. "Yes, ma'am?"

"Would you fix us a nice brunch?"

"I could do eggs benedict real quick."

"That's perfect, thank you."

Anita laughed again. "I was the servant at Daddy's old house and he didn't get fancy eggs on demand." She sipped her drink. "The old bastard was lucky I fed him oatmeal and gave him his damn meds."

"Who picks up trash in Dad's neighborhood?"

"How in hell do I know?" Anita emptied her glass and headed for the bar. "Some company with green and white trucks. They make a lot of noise on Monday mornings."

Robert sat beside his wife on the couch and held up his hand. "That's it!"

"What?"

"Call the county information center. Find out what company has a contract for trash pick up in your dad's neighborhood and what landfill they use. Whatever it is, the nightstand would've been taken there."

Cindy grabbed the phonebook. "It'll be

buried under tons of garbage."

"I have a feeling it won't be."

Anita shook her head. "You two would make a great comedy act." She watched the maid serve their brunch. "Thanks. Would you be kind enough to fix me another martini? That's a good girl."

Robert looked over at Anita slouched at the dining room table. "I hope your father's new will has cut you out altogether."

* * * *

Mr. Thompson rinsed and dried his coffee mug and grinned at the sound of tapping on the side window. "I'll be right there, Sparky." He picked up a plastic bag off his desk and went to the small window.

The fat gray squirrel skittered about on the outside shelf that Mr. Thompson had built for him. The rodent tapped the glass again and barked.

Jim opened the window and scratched Sparky's ears. He was the only human who could ever do that. "I bought fresh walnuts for you last night." He held one out and the animal took it in his paws and began to nibble. "Don't eat so fast, there's plenty for a good lunch." Sparky took another treat from Jim's bare fingers. "We might have to say goodbye soon my friend, but let's not fuss about it just yet." Sparky barked again and chewed on another nut.

The phone rang.

Jim rubbed the squirrel's ears once more. "You know what? If I were a betting man, I'd give you ten-to-one odds that call is about a nightstand or a trunk full of books." He put out five more shelled walnuts and went to answer the phone.

"This is county landfill fifteen. I'm the caretaker, James L. Thompson. How can I help you?"

"Hi, I'm Robert Richards and I have a strange request."

"I get quite a few of those in my business, sir. What is it?"

"Well, we accidentally put out a valuable nightstand for trash collection and we'd like to track it down and get it back. Is that even possible?"

Mr. Thompson sat back and smiled. "Can you describe the item for me?"

"It's white with dark green trim and has one drawer."

"I might have something like that. It came in this morning and I set it aside. Anything else that might help identify the piece?"

"It has hand-painted flowered artwork on its top."

"Mr. Richards, you're having a lucky day. Your nightstand is here."

"Where are you? How do I get there?"

"I'm off Canyon Road North at Mill Road

twenty-two. You can't miss it. I close at five-thirty."

"We'll be there about three."

"I'm looking forward to meeting you."

"Thank you so much."

"You're most welcome."

Jim went back to the window. Sparky was still there. He gave the animal a few more walnuts. "What did I tell you? I won the wager."

The squirrel barked.

* * * *

Robert joined his wife and Anita in the dining room. "They have it at the landfill on Mill Road."

Cindy drew a deep breath. "Thank God."

"I told the caretaker we'd be there by 3:00." He folded the paper with the address and put it in his shirt pocket and glared at Anita. "That should give you enough time to sober up."

"Robert, please."

"Let him rant. He's pissed because the new will might not be in his favor. Isn't that right, Bobby?"

"Did you take a mean-pill along with your booze?"

"That's enough from both of you."

"Your sister's an insolent bitch. She was rude to Karl and treated Jenny with disrespect."

"I'm here—don't talk about me like I'm

not in the same room."

"Actually, Anita, I wish to hell you weren't." He cut into his eggs Benedict and grinned.

She took a sip from her martini and started to get up.

Cindy leaned toward her. "That's it! Sit down. We're going to finish brunch while you drink coffee and get your head straight."

Anita downed the rest of her drink. "You better hope that new will sits right with me or I'll have you both in court and Karl won't be able to hold his ass against me."

Robert wiped his mouth on a fresh linen napkin and smiled, "I guess we're finding out who you really are."

* * * *

Mr. Thompson brought the nightstand into his office, wiped it down and covered it with a large blue towel. "That'll keep it from the dust until they come after it. What do you think, Sparky?"

The squirrel had come back to the window shelf for more treats. He chattered and flipped his bushy tail.

"I thought you'd agree." The caretaker took a handful of walnuts to the open window. "You're sure a hungry little guy or is it something else?"

Sparky ate two of the nuts and started

stuffing his cheeks with the rest.

"That's what I thought. You're feeding a family." He petted Sparky. "I'll bring some peanuts tomorrow. Perhaps you Would like them shelled?"

The animal twitched his tail, held still and then jumped down off the shelf.

A black four door Mercedes stopped in front of the office. Mr. Thompson watched a man and two well dressed women step out. A young looking attractive blonde dropped a cigarette and crushed it out. *She doesn't appear to be too friendly,* he thought. He gestured from the open door for them to come in.

Robert helped Cindy up the four steps. Her sister followed. Mr. Richards smiled, "I'm Robert, we spoke on the phone earlier.

"Pleased to meet you, sir. James L. Thompson at your service." The two men shook hands. "I'm the caretaker."

Robert nodded toward his wife. "This is Cindy, my wife and her sister, Anita."

"My pleasure." The caretaker shook Cindy's hand. She smiled. He reached out to Anita. "Welcome to my humble office."

"Where is it?"

"The nightstand?"

"That's what we're here for."

"I covered it so it wouldn't get dusty." He stepped toward his desk and pulled the towel off the stand.

Anita took two quick strides and yanked

the drawer out of the stand. She turned it over. "It's here!" She tore the envelope off the bottom and dropped the drawer.

Robert shouted, "What the hell are you doing?"

"I want to see what he did."

Cindy grabbed her sister's arm. "This isn't the place."

"It's as good as any." She ripped the flap open and pulled out the document. Anita stepped back and sat in an old leather armchair. "That sonofabitch!"

Robert looked at the caretaker. "I'm sorry about this."

"I'll step outside and let you have some privacy."

"That isn't necessary. We'll be leaving."

Cindy snatched the will away from Anita and stared at it. "Oh, my God."

"What is it?" Robert tried to get a look.

She laughed, "Dad left the house to the county to be used as a nursing home for the elderly."

"I'll be damned."

"Two thirds of all other assets are to be set aside for renovation. The final third is ours." She glanced at her sister, smiled and handed her husband a certified check.

Robert studied the check. "I'm really sorry, Anita."

"Sure you are."

Cindy continued. "There's a note to go with your thousand-dollar check."

"I read it."

Robert nudged his wife. "What did he say?"

"It does hurt a little. Dad wrote; enjoy your inheritance, Anita. Thanks for being the most uncaring caregiver. What goes around comes around, girl. Everything's been notarized and signed."

Anita got up off the armchair. "We'll just have to see about that, won't we?"

Mr. Thompson picked up the drawer and put it back into the nightstand. "I'll take it out to the car for you."

Robert held up his hand. "That's okay, we don't need it."

Cindy stepped forward. "Yes, we do. I want it, thank you."

"What do we owe you?" Robert reached for his wallet.

"Nothing, sir. The nightstand belongs to you. It never should've been here."

"Thank you, I'll carry it out."

Mr. Thompson looked at Anita. "I'm sorry for your loss, ma'am."

She stared at the caretaker with contempt. "Loss? What the hell do you know about loss, junk man?"

"I know you're a beautiful young woman who seems to have lost her heart. I hope you find it before it's too late."

He watched them walk out to the expensive car. Mr. Richards held the back door for Anita. She said, "This isn't over yet."

Robert closed the door and nodded to the caretaker. "I think it's quite over."

* * * *

Mr. Thompson took out his ledger, paged to the end and crossed off the nightstand. *Sometimes, things lost should not be found.* He pondered the thought and put the book away.

The phone rang.

"Mill Road landfill. James L. Thompson. How can I help you?"

"Hello. I hope I have the right place. I got the number from the company that picks up my trash. I pray I'm not too late."

"Too late for what, ma'am?"

"Well, my Grandson and two of his friends cleaned out my attic yesterday. God bless them. They did a bang up job for sure, but the boys made a mistake."

"How so?"

"They brought a trunk full of old books to a recycle center. A nice man there said he took it to your place. My late husband collected all those books and I'd dearly love to have them back."

Mr. Thompson sat back and smiled. "Could you describe the trunk for me?"

"I sure can. It's made of dark brown wood, I don't know what kind. There are metal corners and hinges and leather straps across its flat top."

"I think a trunk like that came in this morning." He grinned and enjoyed the teasing. "It does have some old books inside. Do you remember any of the books in your lost trunk?"

"There's one I know for certain. It was my husband's favorite. He used to call it Old Poe."

Mr. Thompson pulled his chair up to the desk. "Would that be a leather-bound collection of The Complete Works of Edgar Allan Poe?"

"My stars—you have the trunk!" She let out a sigh. "Thank heaven."

"Yes, I do. It's in perfect shape. You can pick it up anytime."

"I'll have my Grandson and one of his friends come by for it." The woman chuckled. "I was afraid I'd never see it again. Thank you so much."

"Actually, your trunk was never really lost. I found it and you found me."

"Now, that's a very nice way of putting it, Mr. Thomas."

"Thompson, Ma'am, James L. Thompson."

"Excuse me?"

"What is it?"

Silence.

"Ma'am?"

Her voice fell to a whisper. "Are you, Jimmy Thompson?"

He held the phone tighter. "My friends call me Jimmy. You may do the same if you like."

"This can't be … Jimmy Thompson?"

He leaned back. "I assure you. That's me. Do I know you?"

"I think you do." The woman took a short breath. "I'm Gayle Martin."

"That doesn't ring a bell, Ms."

"Of course it wouldn't. How silly. That's my married name." She hesitated. "Jimmy, this is Gayle Anne Stewart. We went to high school together. We went steady until after graduation." Her voice cracked. "You went in the Air Force."

Mr. Thompson stared out into the dooryard and watched a swirl of dust and dead leaves whip across the front of his office "Gayle?"

"I'm here. Are you upset?"

"I just caught my breath." A flood of moments lost filled the caretaker's heart. "Your laugh, the look of you, your scent. That smart-ass grin of yours. It all just flooded over me."

"Me too—and the time you dunked me in the pool with my clothes on. You could be a brat."

"You weren't such an angel yourself."

"Is there a Mrs. Thompson?"

Jimmy took a breath and wiped his eyes. "She passed ten-years ago."

"I'm sorry. Any children?"

"I have a son. He's a lawyer and lives in Texas with his wife and their two boys."

"Is there anyone else?"

"I'm alone, Gayle." He laughed. "I have a squirrel friend and a flock of seagulls I feed every day."

"Would you like to see me?"

His voice wavered. "I think that would be the best thing that could ever happen to me."

"Aren't you afraid I'll be big fat and ugly and have false teeth?"

"None of that matters."

"I'm coming over."

"Now? You're coming here?"

"Give me an hour. I have to wiggle into a girdle and put in my dentures."

"Gayle—this is a dump!"

"Doesn't bother me. I'm coming to see you."

"Can we have it all again?"

"You said it yourself. You found my trunk and I've found you. I'm on the way."

* * * *

Mr. Thompson stared out through the open office door and watched the last truck of the day pull to a stop. The driver jumped down from the cab and came in. "I got the shredded green from the golf course." He handed the caretaker his paperwork. "You okay, Jimmy?"

"Yeah, I'm fine."

"You look a little peaked."

"Indigestion from a rushed lunch."

"I hear talk the county's shutting this site down early."

"That's the rumor, Benny."

"Where's that leave you?"

Jim put the yellow invoice in a manila folder. He smiled. "On early retirement, I guess."

"Tough break."

"That all depends on how you look at it."

"Every time you turn around something's changing."

Jimmy got up from his desk. "Always has, I suspect it always will."

"You want my stuff dumped in section twenty-eight?"

"Take it over to thirty."

"Has the county opened that up?"

"No." He grinned, "But I just did."

"You sure about that?"

"Sure as rain."

"It's your ass."

"That it is. You have a good evening and say hello for me to that pretty wife of yours and those spunky kids."

"Take something for that indigestion. It's not good for a man your age."

"Thanks, I appreciate your concern."

* * * *

Mr. Thompson hung his coveralls and work shirt behind the door and looked at himself in the mirror of the cramped bathroom. "Gayle gets one glance at you and she'll turn and run." He clicked on his razor and went to work on his face.

I'll love you forever. He remembered saying those words so many years ago.

He put the razor away and washed up. "Maybe seeing each other isn't such a good idea." He dried on a clean towel and combed what little hair he had left and slipped into a fresh shirt.

Gayle's ancient comment whispered out from a corner of his mind. *Four-years, that's a long time to wait.*

The next memory brought tears to his eyes. *Let's get married now, before I go. After basic training you can come with me.* Gayle's response hung with him for a long time after that day.

I'm only seventeen. I'm not ready for marriage. I love you, but you're a dreamer. Anyway, my parents would never allow it.

He tucked in his shirt and glanced at himself again. "You always were a dreamer and where did it get you?" He put a touch of English Leather on his face. "Maybe she won't show up."

* * * *

Ten minutes later the sun glinted off the windshield of a bright yellow Hummer coming up the road toward the office. The vehicle pulled to a stop and shut down.

Mr. Thompson stood in the doorway trying to swallow the lump in his throat. He whispered,

"This is Gayle?"

The driver's door opened and a tall attractive woman stepped out. "I'm supposed to meet a short chubby old bald man here." She pushed her gray-streaked chestnut hair off her shoulders. "He found a trunk of books I had lost." Gayle's face appeared as radiant as a sunset.

"That gentleman left for the day and put me in charge." His voice started to lose its timber. "He said I should expect a white-haired … old lady … wearing an apron … and orthopedic shoes."

"I lied." Her heart thumped in her ears. "You like my … outfit?" Her eyes glistened.

"You look like … you're going on a … Saturday night hay … ride."

She walked toward him. "I am and with … the most handsome … man on the damn … ranch."

"Gayle I can't … can't find the right words …." He came down off the steps.

"Neither can I … we don't need them."

Silence.

They held each other for a long wonderful moment.

He kissed her with the softness of a warm evening breeze. "I've always loved you, Gayle Anne Stewart."

"And I've always felt the same for you." She leaned back and tapped his nose with her finger. "Don't you ever leave me again, Jimmy."

He laughed. "I didn't leave you. You wouldn't go with me."

"We were just kids. You wanted to get married—I was frightened to death."

"I wanted to be serious."

"Serious?" You were the most intense boy I ever knew." She looked up at him and wiped her eyes. "Are you still that way?"

He hugged and rocked her in his arms. "I've mellowed out quite a bit."

"You know, I was heartbroken. You left me alone and went off on an adventure."

"Alone? I don't think so. There were boyfriends I knew about."

"From whom?" She watched his eyes.

"I heard."

"I'll bet you swept a few dollies off their feet."

"There were a couple." He kissed her nose.

"I love you, Jimmy Thompson."

He held her back and kissed her forehead. "All these years ... I thought you were lost."

"Now we've found each other." She kissed him. "I had a hunch about that old trunk."

"Those books are valuable. I've always wanted to write something like any one of those."

"Maybe now you will."

About the author

Ted Tillotson lives with his family and eight rescued feline friends in Central California. You may contact him through his Web site at: http://www.tedtillotsondragonlairbooks.com